Aubrey leaned into Matt.

"Is there anything else we can do right now? An abandoned building we can stake out? A contact we can lean on for information?"

Matt chuckled. "You don't give up, do you?"

"Not when a little girl's life is at risk."

"I'm not giving up, either." He brushed his thumb over her cheek. "But after what happened this morning and now at the gas station, I'm afraid to take you with me. I'd feel much better if you stayed at the ranch."

Aubrey was shaking her head. "I can't. I don't want to leave any stone unturned. Everyone working on this has a different perspective. We see different possibilities. If I'm not there, what I might have seen in a situation could be the one thing that leads us to the kidnappers."

"You have a point," Matt sighed. "I don't like that you aren't safely tucked away at the ranch, but you have a point."

He lowered his head and captured her mouth with his in a brief kiss.

I finished this book on Mother's Day, missing my mom and my children. My husband and I decided to go to Colorado for a week to enjoy the mountains and the cooler and drier temperatures. It's beautiful here, and I know my mother and children would have loved to be here with me.

I've been blessed to have a wonderful mother who showed me how to love and also how to be independent. She was my friend, my confidant and my strongest supporter. My children are grown now, and I'm blessed by each of them. They are all individuals, strong and beautiful. I loved them from before the day they were born and even more now that they are my best friends.

This book is dedicated to my mother and my children. I love you all so very much.

HIDEOUT AT WHISKEY GULCH

New York Times Bestselling Author
ELLE JAMES

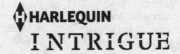

HARLEQUIN
INTRIGUE

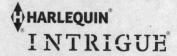

HARLEQUIN®
INTRIGUE®

PLEASE RECYCLE
THIS PRODUCT IS RECYCLABLE

Recycling programs
for this product may
not exist in your area.

ISBN-13: 978-1-335-28446-4

Hideout at Whiskey Gulch

Copyright © 2021 by Mary Jernigan

This edition published by arrangement with Harlequin Books S.A.

For questions and comments about the quality of this book, please contact us at CustomerService@Harlequin.com.

Harlequin Enterprises ULC
22 Adelaide St. West, 40th Floor
Toronto, Ontario M5H 4E3, Canada
www.Harlequin.com

Printed in U.S.A.

Elle James, a *New York Times* bestselling author, started writing when her sister challenged her to write a romance novel. She has managed a full-time job and raised three wonderful children, and she and her husband even tried ranching exotic birds (ostriches, emus and rheas). Ask her, and she'll tell you what it's like to go toe-to-toe with an angry 350-pound bird! Elle loves to hear from fans at ellejames@earthlink.net or ellejames.com.

Books by Elle James

Harlequin Intrigue

The Outriders Series

Homicide at Whiskey Gulch
Hideout at Whiskey Gulch

Declan's Defenders

Marine Force Recon
Show of Force
Full Force
Driving Force
Tactical Force
Disruptive Force

Mission: Six

One Intrepid SEAL
Two Dauntless Hearts
Three Courageous Words
Four Relentless Days
Five Ways to Surrender
Six Minutes to Midnight

Ballistic Cowboys

Hot Combat
Hot Target
Hot Zone
Hot Velocity

SEAL of My Own

Navy SEAL Survival
Navy SEAL Captive
Navy SEAL to Die For
Navy SEAL Six Pack

Visit the Author Profile page at Harlequin.com.

CAST OF CHARACTERS

Matt Hennessey—Former marine and town bad boy, now half owner of the Whiskey Gulch Ranch.

Aubrey Blanchard—Home health-care nurse starting her life over in Whiskey Gulch.

Trace Travis—Former Delta Force who shares his inheritance with his father's bastard son.

Lily Davidson—Girl from the wrong side of the tracks, tainted by her parents' choices in life and in love with the only man she couldn't have. Working as a ranch hand on the Whiskey Gulch Ranch.

Irish Monahan—Former Delta Force soldier who left active duty to make a life out of the line of fire.

Levi Warren—Former Delta Force, left active duty to join Trace and the Outriders, seeking justice for all.

Rosalynn Travis—Trace's mother, recently widowed.

Rodney Morrison—Whiskey Gulch real estate agent.

Sloan Richards—Whiskey Gulch sheriff.

Dallas Jones—Former US Army military police, working as a deputy sheriff in Whiskey Gulch.

Chapter One

"Here's the last of what we had on your mother's case." Sheriff Richards slapped a box marked Evidence on the desk and straightened. "Now, if you don't need anything else from me, I'm late for dinner with my daughter. His brow dipped and he planted his hands on his hips. "Since she learned how to tell time, she doesn't let me off without a firm reprimand."

Matthew Hennessey's lips twisted in a wry grin. "Like father, like daughter?"

The sheriff nodded. "She may look like her mother, God bless her—" he jabbed a thumb toward his chest "—but she's every bit as stubborn as her dad."

"Go," Matt said. "And thanks for digging into this case."

"It's the least we could do. I was on the initial investigation back when your mother was found. There just wasn't a lot to go on. There didn't seem to be a motive. So many people in town loved her. She was always helping others. All we could think of was that she was in the wrong place at the wrong time."

Matt nodded his head. "But out in the middle of a rancher's field?"

"Not far from where she lived. We didn't find any tracks indicating she'd been taken there by a vehicle. Nor did we find any drag marks in the dirt as if she'd been killed at or near her home and then dragged out into the field. It was if she'd gone there on her own and someone shot her there."

Matt frowned at the thought of his mother out at night, alone in a rancher's field. "The ballistics report on the bullet they pulled out showed that she was hit by a bullet from a .45 caliber weapon."

The sheriff nodded. "We checked the registered weapons in the county. Everyone we know who owns a .45 had an alibi."

"The owners might have bad friends who 'borrowed' their guns, though. And I'm sure, the registered guns aren't really the ones you had to worry about," Matt said.

"Right. It was the ones that weren't registered we couldn't account for." The sheriff sighed. "I wish we had more for you."

"Me too," Matt said. "I want to know what happened."

"I understand. If you need anything else, or find something we missed, don't hesitate to contact me. If I'm not available, contact Deputy Jones. I let her know you were looking into your mother's case."

"Thanks." Matt ran a hand through his hair and stretched the kinks out of his back. "Do you mind if I stay awhile?"

"Not at all. No one uses this office, unless they have a long report to write. Things are pretty quiet now, so I don't anticipate anyone needing the space anytime soon." The sheriff gave him a two-fingered salute. "Gotta go."

"That's right. Your daughter is waiting." Matt gave the man a chin lift and focused on the documents in front of him.

Four hours later, the sun had gone down and Matt's belly rumbled. He'd worked through dinner. Not that he had any plans for the meal, but four hours was long enough. In that time, he'd read every word of the depositions, deputies' reports and the state crime lab's detailed analyses of the evidence processed. The medical examiner's report had been the hardest to go over.

His mother had been shot point-blank in the chest, dying instantly. She'd been left in that field until a rancher had noticed turkey vultures flying over her body. He'd gone out to investigate, thinking it might be one of his cows. By the time the man had found Lynn Hennessey, she'd been dead at least two days.

Matt rubbed a hand over his face. Should he head to his apartment over his auto repair shop in town or go out to the Whiskey Gulch Ranch, where he'd moved some of his things into a spare bedroom there?

Matt shook his head. He still couldn't believe he was equal owner of one of the largest and most profitable ranches in Texas, and that he no longer had to work for a living. He had enough money from his father's estate he never had to work another day in his life, other than to keep the ranch running and profitable.

All the years he'd never known who his father was, the man had lived in the same small town where he'd grown up.

All the damned years.

His mother hadn't breathed a word.

Matt might never have discovered his heritage if his mother hadn't died prematurely. His father wouldn't have known of his existence. It all had to do with the letter she'd left with her lawyer, informing James Travis that he'd had a son from their short relationship. If his father hadn't learned of his bastard son before being killed, he would have left his entire estate to his legitimate son, Trace Travis. Instead, he'd left everything to both sons to share equally.

Though he still had vehicles to repair, Matt preferred staying out at the ranch, where the peace and quiet helped him sleep better. Not that Whiskey Gulch was a bustling city with major traffic noise keeping people awake at all hours. But there was the occasional hot rod vehicle cruising down Main Street, mufflers rumbling loudly.

Matt had always dreamed of having a few acres to get lost on. Never in his wildest imaginings had he thought he'd own so much.

It wasn't that he needed to possess anything that had belonged to his father. He would happily have sold his share to his half brother. But his father had bequeathed his entire estate to his two sons. If one of the half brothers wanted out of the ranch, the entire ranch would be sold off and they'd split the proceeds. To keep the property in the family, the ranch had to remain intact and they had to learn to work together. They were doing that, too, and not just concerning the land. With other former military, they'd begun a protective and investigative force that helped victims when law enforcement couldn't quite keep up or provide protection. They'd begun calling themselves "The Outriders." So far, the coalition consisted of Matt, Trace and Irish Monahan, all trained combatants. Soon they'd be joined by others, as they expanded their reach and capabilities.

Matt stacked the documents in a neat pile on the desk, stood and stretched the stiffness out of his muscles. He should have gotten up hours ago to get the blood flowing.

His cell phone buzzed where he'd left it lying on the desk. The caller ID indicated Rosalynn Travis, his stepmother. That word still stuck in his craw. He picked up the phone and answered, "Yes, ma'am."

"Hey, Matthew." Rosalynn was one of the nicest humans Matt had ever encountered, which made it hard for him to hate her. In fact, he liked her tremendously, which gave him twinges of guilt when he thought about the mother he'd loved. And she always called him Matthew, just like his mother had.

Rosalynn continued, "I was just checking to see if you planned on staying at the ranch tonight."

"I am," he said. "I'm leaving the sheriff's office now."

"Oh, good," she said. "Have you had dinner?"

"No, ma'am."

"You don't have to stop on your way to pick up something, if you don't want to," Rosalynn said. "I left pot roast warming in the oven. There's a salad and a fresh pitcher of iced tea in the refrigerator."

"Thank you, Mrs. Travis."

"Matthew, you don't have to call me Mrs. Travis. Rosalynn will do."

"Yes, ma'am."

"And you don't have to call me ma'am." She laughed. "It makes me sound so old."

"Yes, ma'am—Mrs. Travis." He shook his head.

She sighed. "Don't worry about it. We're still getting to know each other. Be careful out tonight. Trace said there were a lot of deer alongside the highway on his way home this evening."

"I'll be on the lookout," he promised, and ended the call.

He stopped at the front desk to let the deputy on duty know he was leaving.

When he stepped out into the night, he looked up at the stars shining brightly overhead.

He'd been many places when he'd been on active duty in the Marine Corps, but nowhere did the stars shine brighter than here in Texas. When a leg injury ended his career as a Marine, he'd come home.

Drawing in a deep breath, he stepped off the curb and mounted his motorcycle, pulled on his helmet and buckled the strap beneath his chin. Matt started the engine and twisted the throttle, giving it some gas while still in neutral. The deep rumble between his legs got his blood moving and his pulse kicking up a notch.

He roared out of the parking lot and onto Main Street, moving slowly as he passed his auto shop, checking for anything out of place. The quiet of Whiskey Gulch was deceiving. Who would have thought anything bad could happen here? Yet, his mother had been shot to death four years ago, and the murderer had never been apprehended. He could still be in the area. He could be one of his neighbors. All the more reason not to trust anyone until he found the killer.

AUBREY BLANCHARD FIT the key in the lock of the cottage, twisted it and pushed the door inward. Her day had been long yet rewarding.

As a home health care worker, she'd gone to six different houses that day to administer to the people who weren't able to take care of them-selves, or who needed a nurse to check on them once a week to draw blood or monitor their vital signs. Unlike her previous job, working in the emergency room of one of Houston's largest hos-pitals, she had time to spend with each patient, listening to their worries and doing the best she could to make them comfortable. Some of them just needed human contact.

She sighed as she entered the home she'd

rented when she'd first come to Whiskey Gulch. It wasn't really a house so much as a cottage, situated on the very edge of town. Behind it was a fenced field where cattle and horses grazed. On the days she got home early, she sat on the covered back porch and watched the sun set over the hills and thanked her lucky stars she'd found the place so quickly after applying for the home health care position she'd found online.

Houston had all the amenities, but it didn't have the peace and quiet Aubrey's soul craved. For the past two months she'd lived here, she'd kept to herself when she wasn't at work. Aubrey needed the space from others, from her own relatives and from her past.

She bent to scoop up the mail on the floor in the entryway that had been shoved through the narrow slot in the door. Among the advertisements for an oil change and a pizza sale was a large envelope with the name of a law firm in the return address.

Aubrey sighed. "It's about time." With the culmination of a yearlong process and thousands of dollars of legal fees, her divorce was final. She didn't have to open the envelope to verify. Her attorney had called a week ago, letting her know of the ruling and that the documents would be coming to her soon. She was a free woman.

A deep sadness filled her for what was, what could have been and what was now her reality.

She tossed the ads, divorce papers and her purse on the antique dining table and headed for the kitchen. Thankfully, the house had come with furniture that had belonged to its last owner. The real estate company that had handled the rental hadn't said a word about what had happened to the last owner. Aubrey assumed she'd died of old age. Three weeks after she'd settled in, Aubrey was corrected on her assumption. One of Aubrey's patients had set her straight on that account. The prior owner had been murdered four years ago.

When Aubrey had heard that bit of news, she'd taken it with a grain of salt. The old woman who'd told her about the owner's murder was suffering from dementia and didn't recognize her own children.

When she'd had a day off, Aubrey had looked the story up on the internet, then gone to the local library and researched area newspapers that had more on the tragedy than online snippets could provide, finding Lynn Hennessey's obituary from four years ago. She went on to locate the article about her death, and how she'd been found in the field not far from her home, shot once in the chest.

Aubrey's belly had knotted. Had she wanted

to get out of her lease agreement on the cottage, she was pretty certain the courts would be on her side. Keeping something as significant as murder from a potential renter had to be grounds for backing out of a contract. By that time, she'd been in the cottage for almost a month. Nothing strange had happened to make her feel unsafe, and the rent was dirt cheap… For a reason. Aubrey had decided the risk was worth it. Since leaving her husband, moving to a new town and establishing a residence, she didn't have a lot of money to burn. So the previous owner had been murdered and the killer hadn't been caught, according to the news article. That didn't mean all occupants of the cottage were destined to be killed.

Armed with the knowledge of Lynn Hennessey's death, Aubrey didn't take any chances. Every night before she went to sleep, she checked all the window and door locks. Not comfortable with guns, Aubrey kept on her nightstand a can of wasp spray capable of shooting bug-killing chemicals up to a distance of ten feet. Anyone who tried to attack her in her own home would get the spray full in the face. She didn't want to kill anyone, just incapacitate potential murderers until she could get far enough away to avoid injury or death.

So far, the can remained untouched. Not even

wasps had made their home in the eaves of the cottage. The house was beautiful, quiet and just what Aubrey had needed after her depressing divorce. She hadn't even ventured out to make friends. Instead, she indulged in solitary evenings at home, drinking wine, catching up on her reading and considering adopting a cat.

That evening was no different. She slipped out of her scrubs and pulled on a pair of leggings and a loose T-shirt, curled up on the overstuffed easy chair and settled in with a book.

The day had been long and tiring. So tiring, she fell asleep on the third page, her wine barely touched.

What felt like moments later, a pounding sound jerked her out of her slumber.

Aubrey sat upright, the book falling from her lap to the floor. The pounding sounded again, but not from the front door. She jumped to her feet and ran for the can of wasp spray in the bedroom before edging around the corner into the kitchen. The back door that led from the kitchen out onto the back porch had a window. A shadowy face pressed against the glass as a fist banged against the wooden doorframe.

The face was female and tear streaked.

Holding tightly to her can of wasp spray, Aubrey hurried to the back door.

"Por favor!" the woman cried. *"Es esta la*

casa de los ángeles?" Her words were so garbled Aubrey had difficulty translating with her rudimentary Spanish skills. She thought the woman was asking for a house of angels.

The tears and the desperation in the woman's voice got to Aubrey. She set the can of spray on the counter, unlocked the door and yanked it open.

The woman fell into her arms, sobbing. *"Ayudar a mis bebés."* Help my babies.

She smelled of sweat and fear. For a moment the woman clung to Aubrey.

"What's wrong? How can I help?" Aubrey asked.

"Mis bebés," she wept. Then she pushed out of Aubrey's arms, grabbed her hand and tugged her toward the door. *"Prisa. Ven conmigo."*

Aubrey resisted. "Where are they? Where are your babies?" she asked, digging her feet into the threshold.

"Por favor. Ayudar a mis bebés."

When Aubrey wouldn't go with her, the woman dropped her hand, ran out into the night, fell to her knees and pressed together her hands in prayer. *"Por favor. Dios ayúdame."* Please. God help me.

Aubrey couldn't disregard the woman's pain. She might be putting her life in danger, but she couldn't ignore the woman's plea. She ran out after her.

When they came to the fence between the cottage's backyard and the rancher's field, the woman slipped between the barbed wire and took off running.

Aubrey stopped cold. This was the field where the Hennessey woman had been murdered. What if the stranger was leading her into a trap? The woman's voice echoed into the night. *"Ayudar a mis bebés."* Help my babies.

Aubrey slipped between the strands of barbed wire. Her shirt ripped on a sharp prong, but she made it through and ran after the disappearing woman, across the field and into a stand of scrubby trees. The land dipped downward into a dry creek bed.

Ahead of Aubrey, the desperate woman slid down the slope and scrambled up the other side.

Aubrey followed. The farther away from the cottage they went, the more her gut knotted. Regretting leaving her phone at the cottage, Aubrey was ready to return and call 911 when the woman stopped in front of a stand of bushes and brush. *"Nena, dónde estas?"* She tore at the branches, pulling aside a large, leafy branch.

A baby's cry sounded in the night. The stranger dived into the brush and emerged with an infant in her arms. *"Marianna, mi bebé."* For only a moment she hugged the infant to her chest, raining kisses on her soft dark hair. Then her head came up. "Isabella?" she whispered.

Aubrey caught up to her.

Holding the baby in her arms, the woman dived deeper into the brush. "Isabella?" she said a little louder.

A child's cry sounded nearby, "*Mamá!*"

The stranger's head whipped around. "Isabella!"

Several engines roared to life, filling the night with a resonating rumble.

Aubrey glanced left, then right, her eyes straining to see into the murky shadows.

The woman who'd led her out into the field shoved her. *"Vamos! Correle más rápido!"* She didn't wait for Aubrey to move, taking off, away from the noise of the engines, clutching her baby to her chest.

For a woman laden with the weight of a small child, she moved fast through the trees.

Even had Aubrey not understood the words, she would have gleaned the intent in her tone. She wanted her to go. To run fast.

A child's cry sounded again over the roar of the engines.

Aubrey turned away from the engines and took off in the direction she'd heard the child's voice.

Ahead of her, the woman's steps faltered. She had to be exhausted after running to get help and then back to find her baby.

Behind Aubrey, dark silhouettes of men on ATVs burst from the shadows and raced toward them.

Aubrey's heart leaped into her throat. She hadn't found the other child, but she was now in jeopardy. If she was going to help, she first had to get to safety.

The stars above shone down on the advancing four-wheelers.

Focusing on the ground in front of her, she ran with all the strength and endurance she could muster.

They'd cut her off from returning to the cottage, so she ran in the only direction she could. Somehow, somewhere, they had to find a place to hide.

Who were these people after this woman? Why were they chasing her? She searched for the words in Spanish but didn't have the time or breath to articulate them.

Aubrey tripped over a branch and fell to her knees. She couldn't get up and run fast enough to avoid the men on the ATVs. She could hide and hope they wouldn't find her, or she could get up and make a stand, giving the other woman and her baby a chance to escape.

Still on her knees, her hand curled around a thick, long stick, bigger than a baseball bat and heavy enough to do some damage.

She waited until just before the ATVs overran her position. It was clear they were aiming at her with harm as their goal.

Aubrey leaped to her feet, and with both hands, she swung the stick as hard as she could at the man on the first ATV to reach her. The stick connected with the man's head, knocking him off the back of the vehicle. He landed flat on his back.

The impact shook Aubrey's arms and wrenched her back. She didn't have time to worry about her own pain.

The second ATV slowed and swerved toward her. The rider's arm came up, a handgun pointing in her direction.

Aubrey ducked behind a tree as a shot rang out.

When the rider roared up to her position, she slid around the other side of the tree and came at him from behind, clobbering him with the makeshift club, hitting him in the head. The man leaned on the right side of his handlebars, sending the ATV careening into a tree.

The third ATV bypassed all of them and continued on toward the woman and the infant.

Aubrey didn't wait around for the two men

she'd hit to gather their wits. She took off again, zigzagging through the trees, heading for the woman who'd broken through the tree line and run across an open field.

Another shot rang out behind her.

Aubrey let out a startled yelp and ran faster. Ahead of her, the man on the ATV raised his arm and fired his handgun.

The woman fell to the ground.

Her steps faltering, Aubrey's heart plummeted to the pit of her belly.

Oh, sweet heaven. Had the woman been hit? What about the baby?

Anger surged through Aubrey, fueling her faltering steps. She ran like a sprinter, winging her way toward the man on the ATV who was bearing down on the woman he'd fired on. As he slowed, Aubrey caught up to him and slammed him with the club-like stick, hitting him in the back of the head.

He slumped over the handlebars of his ATV and shook his head, then he hit the throttle, sending the four-wheeler shooting across the grass, away from his attacker.

A baby's cry drew Aubrey's attention from the rider. When the woman had fallen, the baby had slipped from her arms and landed in a stand of tall grass a yard away.

"Get up." Aubrey tried to help the woman

to her feet. The injured woman didn't have the strength to rise, nor was Aubrey able to carry her.

"Mi bebé. Mi Marianna," the woman cried out, her hand reaching for the child. *"Vamos! Salva a mi bebé!"* Go! Save my baby!

With three men on ATVs chasing her, the woman didn't have a chance. But Aubrey was near a line of trees. If she could reach the trees before the men on the ATVs, she and the baby might have a chance. She would run for help and come back to see if the woman was still alive and look for the other child, as well. Unarmed, she couldn't do much else. The woman wanted to save her baby. That was the least Aubrey could do.

Aubrey scooped the baby into her arms. Her heart pounding, her breathing coming in ragged gasps, she aimed for the trees, pushing herself harder when she thought she could run no more. She didn't look back. Based on the fading engine noises behind her, she was putting distance between herself and the attackers. She prayed she'd make the cover of the trees before the men on the four-wheelers caught up.

Forty yards from her goal, Aubrey heard engines revving. The sound grew nearer. A shot rang out.

Aubrey ducked, fully expecting to feel the sharp sting of a bullet entering her back. When it didn't, she gave everything she had left and ran faster. Her lungs burned, her muscles screamed, but she didn't stop, didn't slow until she entered the shadows of the trees.

Even then, she ran and leaped over small bushes and rotting logs. She'd come too far to give up now. The baby in her arms deserved to live. Aubrey had to stay alive to ensure the child's survival.

Zigzagging through the trees, she debated dropping down behind a pile of brush, but the ATVs following her were getting too close. They'd see her pathetic attempt to hide and be on her immediately. She had to keep moving until she reached a point they wouldn't see her when she dropped out of their line of sight.

Then she came to a barbed wire fence and stopped short of plowing into it with her arms wrapped around the baby. Her heart stopped for several beats. This could be the end of her race, or the break she was looking for.

She shoved the baby between two strands of wire and gently rolled her to the ground. Then Aubrey climbed between the wires, scooped up the baby and took off, hoping the trees on the other side would provide sufficient protection against flying bullets.

Shots rang out again, echoing off the tree trunks.

Hunkering as low as she could, Aubrey kept moving.

The roar of engines behind her faded.

For a moment, Aubrey thought the fence had stopped her attackers.

Then the engines revved again, the sound growing louder by the second. They'd managed to get past the barbed wire and were gaining on her and baby Marianna.

Almost out of energy, Aubrey broke through the other side of the stand of trees and ran out onto a paved road.

A single headlight blinded her.

She held up her free hand, shading her eyes from the glare.

Too exhausted to move another step she dropped to her knees, cupping the baby in her arms, shielding it with her back to the ATV riders and their guns. Her only hope was the driver of the vehicle barreling toward her. The men on the ATVs drove without lights, relying on the starlight to guide them.

Whoever was driving the motorcycle coming toward her had his light on and was on a highway. He could be with the others, but Aubrey took the chance that he wasn't.

She waved her free arm. "Help!" she cried. "Please."

Chapter Two

The woman came out of nowhere.

Matt swerved at the last minute, applied the brakes and came to a screeching halt beside her.

"What the hell?" he called out.

"They're…trying…to…kill me." She staggered to her feet, hampered by the weight of the baby in her arms. "Help us, please."

"Who?" he asked.

Engine noise sounded in the woods.

The woman rushed toward him. "We have to go. Now!"

"Give me the baby and get on the back," he said, scooting forward.

She held tighter to the child, her eyes widening. "No time. Just go! I've got the baby."

"Can you hold on with one arm?"

The racing motors nearby ended any debate. When she slung her leg over the back of his bike, he reached out to steady her and the infant.

With the child sandwiched between them and

her arm around his waist, he took off. A quick glance over his shoulder made his heartbeat sputter.

Behind him, three ATVs burst from the woods and gave chase.

"Hold on!" Matt yelled.

The arm around his waist tightened.

He twisted the throttle, easing it wide-open, giving the motorcycle all the gas it would take.

A crack of gunfire sounded.

Matt leaned into the bike as it sped down the highway, putting distance between them and the woman's pursuers. The high performance Ducati outdistanced the ATVs quickly. Soon, they were out of range of the men and their guns.

Matt didn't slow until he reached the gate to the Whiskey Gulch Ranch, where he decelerated to make sure they were no longer followed. Then he hit the gate remote. When the opening became wide enough, he rolled through. As soon as they were past the wrought iron, he closed the gate and sped down the winding road through the trees to the ranch house.

He stopped in front of the house, where light from the porch shone down on them. Matt waited for the woman to climb off the back before he engaged the stand and dismounted.

"We have to call the sheriff." She looked up from the baby in her arms. "This baby's mother..." Her words were choked off on a sob.

Matt frowned. "This isn't your baby?"

She shook her head. "No."

"Where is the mother?" he asked.

"I think… I think they shot her." She hugged the baby to her chest, tears slipping down her cheeks.

"Matt?" Rosalynn Travis's voice called out from the front porch of the ranch house. "Is that you?"

Matt glanced up at his father's widow. "It's me. I have someone with me. Get the sheriff on the phone. We have an emergency."

"Oh, my," she said. "What's wrong?"

The baby let out a pathetic whimper.

"I'm not sure, but I think someone was shot," Matt called out.

His half brother, Trace, stepped out of the house behind his mother, with his fiancée, Lily, by his side. "Who was shot?" Trace asked.

"I'm not sure." He slipped a hand around the woman's shoulders. "Come inside. We'll get the sheriff on the phone."

"We have to hurry," the woman said. "She might still be alive."

He hustled her up the steps and into the house.

Rosalynn Travis held a cordless phone to her ear. "Yes, I'd like to report a shooting, I think." She looked to Matt and shrugged. "I'm not sure where. Hold on."

The woman who'd ridden on the back of his motorcycle leaned the baby up on her shoulder and reached out with her freed hand, tear tracks on her cheeks. "Here, let me."

Rosalynn handed her the phone.

As the woman took the phone and drew in a deep breath, Matt studied her.

She was fairly new in town. He recalled seeing her a couple times, coming and going from the grocery store across from the auto shop. He'd been curious about the new girl in town with the pretty auburn hair. Too busy with his shop and working with his half brother to figure out who'd killed his father, he hadn't had the time to introduce himself. Standing near her in the house he'd inherited with Travis, he could see that she had soft, moss-green eyes.

"This is Aubrey Blanchard. I rented the cottage on Maple Street on the edge of town."

Matt stiffened. Maple Street. He'd grown up in a house on Maple Street, at the edge of town. His mother had owned the house there. After her death, he'd placed the house with a lease management company. He didn't have the heart to sell it, nor did he have the heart to live in it after his mother had been killed. The place held too many memories that overwhelmed him every time he walked through the door. He could swear it still smelled of her perfume and he could hear echoes of her voice.

"A woman banged on my door crying a little while ago." Aubrey's words came out in a rush. "She was speaking Spanish, begging me to help her save her babies. When I followed her out into the field behind the house, she led me to where she'd hidden her baby in the brush. She was looking for another child when we heard the child's cry. That's when three men on ATVs burst out of the woods and chased us. They shot the woman. She told me to take the baby and run." Her grip on the phone tightened until her knuckles turned white. "I couldn't go back to help her." Aubrey's voice cracked. "I had to save…the baby." Her shoulders shook. "Please. We have to go back. She could still be alive. And the other child—" she swallowed hard "—we have to find the other child."

Lily gasped.

Rosalynn pressed her hand to her mouth. "Poor dear."

The baby in Aubrey's arms squirmed and let out a cry. Aubrey shoved the phone toward Matt and held the child in the cradle of both her arms. "Oh, sweetie, I'm so sorry."

Matt pressed the phone to his ear. "This is Matt Hennessey. Who am I talking to?"

"Deputy Jones," a female voice responded.

"I found Ms. Blanchard on the highway," Matt said. "I'm not sure exactly where, but I can meet you at the house she lives in on Maple Street in ten minutes."

"I'll notify the sheriff and we'll be there as soon as possible," Jones said. "Be careful. The men who attacked Ms. Blanchard could still be around."

As Matt ended the call, the baby's whimpers turned into a wail.

"Aubrey, I'm Rosalynn Travis. You've met Matt, my stepson." Rosalynn turned to Trace and Lily. "This is my son, Trace, and his fiancée, Lily." She held out her arms. "Here, let me have the baby. It's probably hungry, wet and scared."

"Marianna, I think that's what her mother called her," Aubrey said, as she handed over the crying baby. "The other child's name was Isabella. Her mother called her name several times before the little girl cried out." Aubrey looked up at Matt. "We have to go back. That little girl must be terrified. She could be lost out there." She touched his arm. "What if those men took her, or…killed her?" Her gaze went to baby Marianna. "We have to go back."

Matt caught Trace's glance.

"We'll go," Matt said.

Trace nodded. "I'll get Irish. We can offer

our assistance to the sheriff in the search for the mother and the other child."

"I'll go," Lily said.

"I'm going too," Aubrey said.

Matt shook his head. "Those men were playing for keeps. You two are better off staying here and helping Rosalynn with the baby."

Lily's eyes narrowed. "I know how to handle a gun. You might need more firepower."

Aubrey lifted her chin. "I might not know how to use a gun, but I have to go. I know where this all began. I can lead you to where she found the baby and to where she fell to the ground. I'm your best chance of finding her quickly." She stared up at him, her brow furrowed. "I have to go. *We* have to go. *Now*."

"She has a point," Trace said.

"But she won't be safe. If those ATV riders are still out there, they might consider her a threat."

"I only left because I had to get the baby to safety," Aubrey said.

"I'll take care of the baby," Rosalynn said. "You guys get out there and find her mother."

"I thought I heard voices." Irish appeared at the door and entered. "What's going on?"

"We need to go," Trace said. "Grab your rifle and a handgun and meet me at my truck. I'll fill you in on the way." He turned to Aubrey. "You can ride with us."

She looked from Matt to Trace and back. "If it's okay with you, I'd like to ride with him." Aubrey tipped her head toward Matt.

He liked the idea more than he cared to admit. "I have an extra helmet in my room. I'll be right back." Matt climbed the stairs, two at a time, hurrying to the room he'd moved some of his things into. He grabbed the extra helmet from a shelf in the closet and the handgun he kept in the nightstand, slipping the pistol into the pocket of his leather jacket. He was back by her side in less than two minutes.

"Ready?" he said.

She nodded, her brow furrowed. "We need to hurry."

"We will." He looked around for Trace and Irish.

Rosalynn called out from the living room. "The boys and Lily are on their way to the cottage where Aubrey lives. They figure you'd catch up with them pretty quickly."

Matt hooked Aubrey's arm and escorted her out of the house.

She looked over her shoulder as she left.

Rosalynn waved a hand. "Don't worry about us. I have experience raising babies."

"That's more than I can say," Aubrey murmured. "I only raised one."

Outside, in the light from the porch, Matt

stopped next to his motorcycle. "Here, you need to wear this." He slipped the helmet over her head and tightened the strap beneath her chin. Then he climbed on and tipped his head. "Hop on and hold on tight."

She did as he indicated, slipping her leg over the seat. She scooted close and wrapped both arms around his waist.

Matt started the engine and took off down the drive toward the gate. Thankfully, Trace had left it open. He drove right through and opened the throttle.

The woman behind him held tightly to him, her arms cinched around his middle, her legs clamped around his thighs. He liked the way she felt, coupled with the rumble of the engine between his legs. If they weren't in a hurry to save the lives of a woman and a child, he would have made the drive last longer.

A mile before they reached town, he caught up with Trace in his pickup, passed him and sped on to the cottage on Maple Street. It was the same house he'd grown up in. The house he'd shared with his mother until he'd left Whiskey Gulch to join the Marine Corps. It was the house he'd come back to when he'd learned of his mother's murder.

Two law enforcement SUVs were parked at the curb. Sheriff Richards and Deputy Dallas

Jones were getting out of their vehicles when Matt pulled into the driveway, stopping behind a gray Jeep Wrangler.

Trace drove his pickup beside him, cut the engine and got out with Irish and Lily doing the same, joining the group.

When Aubrey started toward the house, the sheriff said, "Wait. Let us go first." He and Deputy Jones had pulled their weapons and started toward the door.

"The front door is locked," Aubrey said. "I left through the back."

Sheriff Richards tipped his head to the right. "I'll go right."

The deputy rounded the house to the left. A quick minute later, they exited through the front door.

"Clear," Deputy Jones reported.

"Follow me." Aubrey took off around the house and through the backyard, crossing to the fence bordering the rancher's field beyond. The stars above provided sufficient light for them to see without flashlights.

Aubrey didn't stop there. She ducked to slide between two strands of barbed wire.

Matt pulled the strands wider to keep them from snagging her shirt or skin. When she was through, he braced his hand on the post and vaulted over the fence. The others followed.

Aubrey started running toward a stand of trees on the other side of the field.

"Wait," he said, hurrying to catch her. "If they're still out there, they could pick you off in a field as wide-open as this one."

"But we have to get there. Marianna's mother could still be alive. If we don't hurry, she could bleed out." Aubrey tried to shake free of his hand.

"Let us go ahead. We're trained in combat— you aren't."

"I'll stay with her," Lily said. The two women dropped to their haunches and waited.

"I'll signal with two blinks of my flashlight when you can join us," Matt said.

The men and Deputy Jones moved ahead swiftly, their weapons drawn, hunkering low to avoid being shot, should the perpetrators be aiming in their direction.

When they reached the shadows of the tree line, the sheriff pulled them together. "I know you guys are trained in combat but you're civilians here. Let us take the lead." He took the deputy and moved forward. Irish, Matt and Trace fanned out, searching the darkness beneath the canopy of foliage for men, ATVs or a woman and her child. When they found nothing, Matt aimed his flashlight back across the field and blinked it twice.

He covered the two women as they ran across the field. When they caught up, Aubrey's head turned right, then left. "It was all a blur. I don't know exactly where she'd hidden the baby…" She slid down into a creek bed and back up the other side and then walked to a pile of brush where a loose limb with leaves lay on the ground. "I think she'd hidden the baby in here." Aubrey disappeared into the brush.

Matt's pulse ratcheted up. He was about to go in after her when she emerged with a large, woven bag.

"This was where she'd left her baby and her other child. After she came out with Marianna, she called out for Isabella." She looked around, her shoulders hunching. "That's when they came out of the trees on four-wheelers."

"Do you know how old Isabella might have been?" the sheriff asked.

She shook her head. "I can only assume she was a toddler or bigger, since the baby could only be a few months old." Aubrey moved away from the brush in the opposite direction of the cottage, her steps quickening until she was almost running, moving around fallen logs and brush. When she emerged into a field, she gasped and tore out.

Matt caught up and sprinted with her to where

she fell on her knees beside a dark lump on the ground.

"Oh, sweet heaven," she cried, and reached toward the dark object.

Matt grabbed her hands before she could lay them on the body of a woman, lying in the dirt, facedown, a bullet hole in her back.

The sheriff was there beside them. He rolled the woman onto her back. The hole in her back was small compared to the damage the bullet had made on its exit. Her shirt was saturated in her blood, her face a waxy blue in the starlight.

Matt knew before the sheriff confirmed it what the verdict would be.

The sheriff did what he had to do, pressing his fingers to the base of the woman's throat. For a long moment he remained still. Finally, he shook his head. "No pulse. I'm afraid she's dead."

Tears streamed down Aubrey's face. "She was trying to save her children." Her tears stopped and her eyes widened. "Isabella. We have to find Isabella." She struggled to her feet and turned, her gaze searching for the missing child. "Isabella!" she called out.

"We need a search party," the sheriff said. He got on his radio and notified dispatch.

"You don't have enough people on your staff to man a search party," Matt said.

"No, but we have a telephone tree of volunteers in case of fire," the sheriff said. "They'll help with a missing person. And I know someone with a search and rescue dog."

Within the next hour, Sheriff Richards's call garnered more than a hundred people. When the volunteers had heard a child was missing, they phoned their friends and their friends phoned their friends. They came out in droves to help in the search for the missing girl.

While they were waiting, the sheriff, deputy, Irish, Matt and Trace spread out looking for the ATVs and the shooters. The last thing they needed was for the volunteers to become the next victims.

By the time the volunteers had arrived, they'd determined the men on the ATVs had gone. In their search, they hadn't found the little girl. Matt feared the child was lying in the brush dead. If she wasn't dead, she might be frightened out of her mind and afraid to come out with all the strangers wandering around.

The SAR dog, a German shepherd, and his handler arrived with the others. While the volunteers were organized into a line stretching out for several hundred yards, the sheriff pulled from the satchel they'd found items of clothing too big for the baby and more suitable for a small girl of three or four years old. He held them in front of the German shepherd's nose. The dog sniffed and went to work in the woods where the mother had hidden her children.

It wasn't long before the dog lost the scent. He kept returning to the brush pile.

"The girl was here," his handler said. "But she didn't walk out on her own."

Aubrey's body shook. "They took her."

Matt slipped an arm around Aubrey and pulled her close against him. The shock of all that had happened would be setting in. He was surprised she was still standing on her own.

"We have to find her," Aubrey said.

"We will," Matt promised. As he made the promise, he wondered how the hell he would keep it. They didn't know who the men on the ATVs were, or why they would take a small child and kill her mother.

Chapter Three

Aubrey leaned into Matt Hennessey, whose arm rested firmly around her waist. So much had happened that night. Tremors still shook her, making it hard for her to stand on her own. Somewhere out there a little girl was missing her mother. Aubrey's heart ached for the girl. "I need to help in the search."

"No, you don't. There are enough people out here. If the girl is in the field or in the woods, they'll find her," Matt said.

"How can they find what the dog wasn't able to locate?" Aubrey whispered. "She's gone." Her chest tightened. "Now that I think about it, they might have had her before we got to the baby." She looked up at the man keeping her from falling to her knees. "Why? Why would they take a small child and shoot her mother?"

He didn't respond. He didn't have to.

Aubrey knew why men stole children. Every day in the news there was something about human trafficking, young girls being sold into sex slavery, pedophiles preying on their young victims and the rape and murder of the helpless. A sob rose up her throat. She swallowed hard to keep from releasing it. She knew firsthand what happened to little girls. "We have to find her." She pushed away from Matt and started toward the line of people combing the field and woods for a little girl they wouldn't find. Not here. The men on the ATVs had taken her somewhere else. But where?

Matt hooked her arm, bringing her to a halt.

She stared up at him. "You don't understand. The first forty-eight hours are the most crucial," she said. "If we don't find her by then, we may never find her, or…we'll find her body in a ditch."

Matt tipped her chin up. "You have to have faith that we'll find her."

"I know the odds. They aren't good." She stepped out of the man's grip, her shoulders going back. "Searching this field is a waste of time. We have to find the men on the ATVs. We can't wait. The longer we wait, the farther away they'll take her."

"We need to give them time to search the area. They might find some evidence of who the men were on the four-wheelers."

Anger, fear and desperation bubbled up inside

Aubrey. "You don't understand. They're wasting time. Those men took that little girl. Her life is in danger. The longer we stand around here the less likely she'll make it to her next birthday." A sob lodged in her throat. Her own little girl hadn't made it to her fourth birthday. Taken from her front yard when Aubrey's back was turned, her Katie had been stolen and taken away. Not only had her abductor stolen the child, he'd stolen her life, snuffing it out as soon as he'd used up her little body.

"Please," Aubrey begged. "Help me find her."

"Okay," Matt said. "Let's talk with the sheriff. Maybe he's discovered her mother's identity. That might lead us to who would have targeted her and her children."

He guided her over to where the sheriff stood beside the body being loaded onto a stretcher.

"We'll transport her to the local coroner for an autopsy, but it's pretty clear she was shot, like Ms. Blanchard stated."

"Did you find out who she was?" Matt asked.

The sheriff held up a bag. "All we could find that might give us a clue is a wallet we discovered in the big satchel. It contained some US money and some Mexican pesos. There was a photograph of what appeared to be our victim and a few other adults around the same age. Maybe family members. And there was a piece of paper with an address of someone in the small town of Hico. I scanned the photograph on my smart phone and sent it to my contact with the Texas State Police. I told them our victim could be an illegal immigrant. They're sending someone in plain clothes to the address."

Aubrey nodded. "Good. Apprehending illegal aliens isn't what we need to be doing right now. We need to know who the woman was and why she would be targeted. We have to find her killers. They have Isabella."

"I've considered that. But I can't call off the search here until we know for sure," Sheriff Richards said. "If that little girl is out in the woods, she has more than a few ATV killers to worry about. Snakes, coyotes of the four-legged kind, and we've had some sightings of mountain lions in this area." He held up his hand. "But don't worry, we're not just looking here. I have a couple of my deputies setting up roadblocks on the main highways and secondary feeders in and out of Whiskey Gulch, watching for vehicles passing through the area."

Aubrey shook her head. "I just know…it's too late. We have to figure out who would have done this. Finding one person responsible would be hard. Three attackers should make it easier. They couldn't have gone far on their ATVs before they transferred to another, faster vehicle." She focused all of her thoughts on saving the little girl as she paced in front of the sheriff. "Either they had to ditch the off-road vehicles somewhere, or they loaded them on trailers and shipped them out of here."

"We thought of that," the sheriff said. "We're hampered by night. If we had daylight to work with, we could put a chopper in the air and look for a truck and trailer. Since there were three ATVs, the trailer had to be big enough for all three, maybe four if they had already snatched the child. Or they could have had a tractor trailer rig staged to load into on a highway nearby."

The sheriff's radio crackled. "Excuse me," he said, and stepped away from Matt and Aubrey.

Aubrey strained to hear what the call was about and the sheriff's response.

Matt stood beside her, his attention on the sheriff, as well.

"They did? And?"

Aubrey had trouble making out the words through the static of the radio. She caught every other word.

"…legal…immigrated…paid…coyote."

Coyote.

She knew that term from news reports. Coyotes were the evil men who extorted money from desperate people to bring them across the Mexican-American border. Many times, they killed them, left them to starve or die of thirst or traded them to human traffickers.

The sheriff turned back to Aubrey. "Did you hear all that?"

Her heart lodged firmly in the pit of her belly, Aubrey nodded. "Enough. I think I get the gist."

"The woman was Rosa Martinez. Her brother paid a coyote to get his sister and her family out of a town overrun with a drug cartel after her husband was murdered in the streets. The coyote was to bring them to Hico, where they would hire an immigration attorney and attempt to get her citizenship."

Her heart ached for the mother and the little girls who would never know her. "She didn't make it."

An arm slipped around her shoulders. "No, but her baby will," Matt reminded her. "Because of you."

"And her little girl," Aubrey reminded him. "We have to find Isabella."

"And Isabella."

For another hour, the volunteers searched the field, the woods and the field on the other side of the stand of trees.

Halfway through the search, they found a child's small jacket and the knobby tire tracks of a four-wheeler. The sheriff had the deputy snap photos of the tracks and the jacket as it was found.

The SAR dog was brought to the location to sniff the jacket. Once again, the dog lost the scent immediately.

"They took her on one of the four-wheelers. My Ruger would have found her if she'd been on her own two feet," the dog handler said.

Just in case the abductors had dumped the child farther away from where they'd snatched her, the sheriff had the volunteers continue to comb the fields and woods. By then, it was well past midnight.

"We'll come back out in the morning to see if we can follow the tracks to where they met up with transport out of here," the sheriff said. The volunteers dispersed, leaving the sheriff, the deputy, Matt, Aubrey, Trace, Lily and Irish.

"You might as well go home and get some rest," Sheriff Richards said. "We'll reconvene our search when we have daylight to work in." He frowned when he looked toward Aubrey. "You might want to stay somewhere else tonight. If the kidnappers were after both children, they might take it personally that you cost them the money they could have gotten for the baby. Coyotes don't take the loss of money lightly."

"Have you had many coyotes working in this

area?" Matt asked. "I never hear of them except around Laredo or Juárez."

"Because they stay so far beneath the radar, you don't know they're out there," the sheriff said. "Most of them just get their paying customers across the border. Then the immigrants are on their own to make it to safety."

"Why Whiskey Gulch?" Matt asked. "It's not even that close to the border."

"People coming across try to keep moving inland from the border," Deputy Jones said. "They're probably passing through Whiskey Gulch to Dallas or farther north. We've had several cases over the past year of ranchers finding people passed out on their property from dehydration or hunger. The people are desperate, but not desperate enough to ask for help. They're afraid they'll be turned over to the CBP and returned to their country, where they have nothing."

"But they have nothing here," Aubrey argued.

"Yes, but, for the most part, they aren't being used for target practice here."

"Until Rosa and her daughters?"

The sheriff's lips thinned into a grim line. "Actually, we found another body recently in a ditch a couple miles south of here. A female, also shot in the back. She had a backpack filled with clothing for herself and a child. We found no other bodies nearby. We assumed she was alone."

Aubrey drew in a sharp breath. "Those men could have killed her and taken her child, as well."

"In her case, she seemed to be heading for the town of Whiskey Gulch. Whether she was passing through or planned on stopping, we don't know," the sheriff said.

"We found a folded sheet of paper in her clenched fist with something written in Spanish on it," the deputy said. "Translated it was *house of the angels*."

A chill rippled through Aubrey even though the Texas night was still warm. She looked from the sheriff to the deputy. "*Casa de los ángeles?*"

The deputy nodded. "Yes. Exactly."

For a moment, Aubrey forgot how to breathe. It was as if the ghost of Rosa Martinez was whispering in her ear.

Matt tightened his arm around her shoulders. "What's wrong?"

She looked up into his piercing dark eyes, wanting to brush back the strand of dark hair that had fallen down over his forehead. She blinked twice to regain focus. "When Rosa was banging on my door, she was yelling something." Drawing in a deep breath, she repeated the woman's entreaty, "*Es esta la casa de los ángeles?*"

Matt frowned. "She asked you if the cottage was the house of angels?"

Aubrey nodded. "Yes. I understood the words, but they didn't make sense to me at the time." She sighed. "They still don't. What did she mean by asking me if the cottage on Maple Street was the house of angels?"

"That she asked and the dead woman from a couple weeks ago had the same words on a note is too much of a coincidence," the sheriff said.

Matt shook his head. His gut was telling him it wasn't a twist of fate. "I don't believe in coincidence. The two murders are obviously related. Two women were murdered, and their children taken. These men are stealing children. The question is where are they taking them?"

"And who they're selling them to," Deputy Jones said.

"Do you think they're taking them to the house of angels?" Aubrey asked.

The sheriff's eyes narrowed. "You say Rosa Martinez asked you if your cottage was the house of angels?"

Aubrey nodded. "That's what it sounded like. I could have remembered it wrong. Everything happened so fast, and she was crying."

The sheriff shoved a hand through his hair. "I'll put out some feelers to some of my local Hispanic contacts and see if they know something we're missing." He sighed. "In the meantime, I need to catch a few hours of sleep and get back out here at sunup when the volunteers are due to arrive."

"We'll be here," Trace said. Irish and Lily nodded.

Matt didn't respond. He'd be where Aubrey was, and he guessed it wouldn't be looking through a field for a missing girl. She was convinced the girl was long gone. He tended to agree with her. However, the search effort would be worth it, if they found a clue as to who had taken the girl.

"Had enough wind in your ears?" Trace asked Aubrey. "Wanna ride back to the ranch in the truck?"

Aubrey looked to Matt. "I'd prefer to ride with Mr. Hennessey, if he doesn't mind."

He shrugged. "Not a problem. And you can call me Matt." Secretly, he was glad she'd agreed to ride with him. After rescuing her from the bad guys, he felt responsible for her well-being. They walked back through the woods and across the fields to the cottage, where Trace, Lily and Irish loaded into the truck and left for the ranch.

Aubrey stood next to Matt's motorcycle with her arms wrapped around her middle as if she was cold.

When Matt held out her helmet, she shook her head.

She backed a step. "You don't have to take me back to your ranch. I'll stay at the cottage."

What the hell was she thinking? Now Matt shook his head. "You can't stay here by yourself. If those guys figure out who you are, they might be back to get revenge for having interfered with their human trafficking operation."

"In that case, I don't want them to follow me to the ranch where the baby is."

"By now, the baby will have been taken by Child Protective Services," Matt reasoned. "I heard the sheriff talking with dispatch. Even if they haven't collected the baby, there are enough people at the ranch to protect her and you."

"I don't need protecting. I can take care of myself."

Matt smiled. "You did last time. They won't be surprised this time. Three to one is not the best odds." He raised his eyebrows. "Do you even own a gun?"

She bit her bottom lip. "No."

"How will you defend yourself?"

"I'll lock the doors and windows," she said.

"They can break those down."

She lifted her chin. "I have a can of wasp spray that will shoot a stream up to ten feet."

"That would be great if all you were up against

was an angry wasp." Matt shook his head again. "These guys killed a woman. Don't be their second victim for tonight. You have to stay alive long enough to help me find Isabella."

"How are we going to find her?" Aubrey asked. "We don't know who took her, and the only person who might have identified them is dead."

"Those guys had to have taken the girl to a place close by. With the sheriff having put up blockades on all the roads leading into and out of Whiskey Gulch, they have to eventually go through."

"How do you know he didn't already go through while we were scouring an empty field looking for a child that wasn't there?" Aubrey asked.

Matt held up his hands. The woman was stubborn. "Look, I don't want to argue with you. I can't leave you here alone. Either you come with me to the ranch and be surrounded by men trained in combat who can and will protect you… or I'll be forced to stay here with you."

Her brow wrinkled. "You won't be forced to stay anywhere. I'm not asking you to stay. You can go back to the ranch and leave me here."

He shook his head firmly. "Sorry. I can't do that."

"But I didn't ask you to stay," she said. "I didn't invite you into my home."

"If you don't let me in, I'll camp out on the deck." He crossed his arms over his chest and stood with his shoulders back, his feet spread wide, ready for battle. "Either way, I'm not leaving you alone."

Aubrey opened her mouth as if to tell him where he could go. She must have thought better of it because she closed it again. "Okay. Fine. You can sleep in the spare bedroom. For the record, I don't have a habit of inviting strangers into my home."

"For the record—" Matt closed the distance between them and tilted her chin up with the tip of his finger "—I don't make a habit of sleeping with strangers." His lips twitched. "Not that I'll be sleeping with you."

"Damn right you won't be sleeping with me," she said, her voice a little breathy.

"I'm glad you agree. It would have been awkward if you showed up to my room later in the evening." He grinned.

She snorted and stepped away. "Not happening."

"Didn't expect it." He winked. "Come on. Don't get all defensive. I'm giving you a hard time. That's all. You know…sarcasm?" He laid her helmet on the bike's seat. "By the way, you're cute in the helmet. All you need are some leathers and you'll look like a regular biker babe. And no… I'm not flirting. Just making a statement."

She frowned. "I'm not interested in becoming a biker babe. I'd never been on one until you found me and Marianna on the highway."

"For someone who'd never been on a motorcycle, you did good leaning into the curves." He tilted his chin toward the house. "Wanna show me to the room I'll be sleeping in?"

Her brow knit. "I guess. Though I still think it's overkill for you to stay."

"Rather overkill than roadkill." He grinned. "I crack myself up."

Aubrey rolled her eyes. "You're a regular comedian. You can park your bike in the shed behind the house in case it rains. That's where I usually park my Jeep. Come on. I need to move it into the shed anyway."

Matt pushed the bike around to the structure in the back of the house.

Aubrey ran into the house, grabbed her keys and drove her Jeep out to the shed. The door was unlocked. She parked her vehicle to one side, allowing room for his motorcycle. Other than a couple of shovels and a rake, there wasn't much anyone would want to steal.

Matt waited at the door. "I called to let the others know we wouldn't be coming to the ranch tonight."

"Thank you," she said and stepped outside. "There's enough room in here for your bike."

Matt pushed the bike in beside the Jeep and set it up on its kickstand. As he left the building, he closed the door behind him.

Aubrey led the way to the front door of the cottage Matt knew like the back of his hand. He'd sworn when he left Whiskey Gulch, he'd never come back to stay. Ironic how his life had turned out. Had he not been injured and medically retired from the Marines, he might have kept his promise to himself. Something about his mother's death had brought him back to stay in the town he'd never wanted to see again.

When Aubrey started to reach for the door handle, Matt brushed aside her fingers, feeling a spark of electricity that gave him pause. What the hell? She was just a woman who'd jumped out in front of him on a deserted highway. Nothing more. He'd do well to keep his head and heart in the game. A child was missing. He'd work with Ms. Blanchard to find the child. Then he'd go back to his auto repair business and the ranch. He had enough to do without adding a female to the mix. In his books, they were all drama and hard work for little return.

But, if he was in the market for a woman, Aubrey Blanchard wouldn't be a bad choice. She was strong, having carried a baby on the run.

She was courageous. Hell, she'd taken on three killers on ATVs without worrying about her own safety. All to save a stranger and her children.

Her slender figure, auburn hair and green eyes were a bonus. And when she'd wrapped her arms around his waist, he couldn't deny how good it felt to have feminine hands on him. Maybe it was time to get back into the dating scene. He'd avoided it when he returned to Whiskey Gulch, not wanting to relive the drama he'd experienced in high school. Living in a small town, everyone knew everyone else. Gossip was the only entertainment.

Matt hadn't been interested in rekindling any of his old flames. He'd been out in the world, seen things he could never forget and had only wanted to keep a low profile and blend into the woodwork.

The women who'd stayed in Whiskey Gulch after high school didn't attract him in the least. They still considered him the bad boy he'd been in school. And that was only because of the way he'd dressed. Matt hadn't committed any crimes. He'd only *looked* like he could. His mannerisms and reputation got him in trouble on more than one occasion with the cops and with protective fathers. It had even gotten him sideways with his half brother, though he hadn't known how sideways until recently. Thankfully, he and Trace had smoothed out their differences and were establishing some semblance of a working relationship in order to keep from selling the ranch.

Matt pushed open the door and stepped over the threshold into his past with a hard kick to the gut.

Chapter Four

Aubrey almost ran into Matt's back.

The man stopped and froze in place as soon as he stepped inside the cottage.

"What?" she asked, trying to look around him to determine why he'd made a complete halt. "Is it safe?"

The cottage was small with an open concept living area leading to the kitchen. A breakfast bar and stools provided the delineation between the two rooms.

Matt rolled his shoulders back and stood a little taller. "Sorry. It's just that nothing has changed in this room since the last time I—"

"You've been in this house before?" Aubrey asked, her curiosity peaking. The fact he'd been here didn't bother her; it made her feel a little closer to this man. "What was the former owner like? I mean, all the furniture was here when I rented it. Thankfully. I had nothing."

He didn't answer for a long moment, his gaze

going to every corner of the living room, pausing with the paintings on the wall. Finally, he said, "She was good."

Aubrey slipped around him. "That's what I get from those who knew her. Lynn Hennessey." Aubrey frowned. "Wait. I heard you tell the sheriff's deputy your name was Matt Hennessey." She tilted her head. "Are you and Lynn related? Was she your wife?" Her heart fluttered.

Matt shook his head.

Aubrey's heartbeat returned to normal.

"She was my mother," Matt said.

Her gut clenched. "Oh, Matt. I'm so sorry." She looked around the living room, as if seeing what he saw. "Staying here must be very hard for you." She stepped toward the door. "Look, I'll go with you to the ranch. We can stay out there."

"No," he said, his jaw tight. "We're here now. We might as well call it a night, or what's left of it."

Aubrey could feel the man's pain all the way to her bones. "I'm being selfish. It would be better if we stayed at the ranch," she insisted.

Matt turned to her. "My mother has been gone for four years. I'm okay." He didn't look okay. His lips were pressed in a thin line and his hands were clenched into fists.

A thought made her stomach knot even harder. "Was this your home, too?" she whispered.

He nodded. "My mother brought me here when I was young. This town was her home. Even when she lived away, she always wanted to come back."

Aubrey waved a hand toward the furnishings. She hadn't changed much, other than adding a couple of accent pillows and lap blankets. "And these were her things?"

Again Matt nodded. "They were." He walked deeper into the cottage, pausing to stare at the painting of a water jug full of cut pink tulips on the wall. "She loved this painting." He huffed out a soft breath. "She said it gave her joy to look at it. I think it looks like a bunch of dead flowers that will shrivel and die. But it made my mother happy."

Aubrey hadn't given the painting much thought, only that it did make her smile when she passed it in the hallway. "It's like it welcomes me home after a hard day's work."

"What kind of work do you do?" Matt asked.

"I'm a home health care nurse," she said, moving past him to straighten a cushion on the couch. Knowing the place had been his mother's gave Aubrey a whole new perspective on it and a lot more pressure. Was she keeping it as clean as his mother had? Had she damaged any of the lovely antique furniture his mother had obviously loved dearly?

"I'd heard they'd rented her place," Matt said. "I thought it was to an old woman. Definitely someone from out of town. Who else would rent a house where the former owner had been—"

When he stopped in midsentence, Aubrey finished it for him with, "Murdered?" She gave him a gentle smile. "No one told me about that little detail. Not that it made a difference, once I found out. From what the newspaper reported, she didn't meet her demise in this house."

"No, but the entire town considers this place jinxed or something. No one wanted to live here after she was gone," he said softly. "She loved this house. It was hers. She worked hard to pay it off in fifteen years. Sometimes, she worked two jobs just to make double payments."

He shook his head. "She should have spent that extra money on enjoying her life, traveling or buying pretty things instead of old furniture she had to strip and refinish."

Aubrey looked around the room. "But the things she furnished this house with are priceless. And so very well taken care of. I do my best to be gentle with them. I could tell that whoever they belonged to had cared for and polished them. I could do no less." Her gaze swept the room, taking in the oval Queen Anne coffee table, its wood stained a pretty cherry and polished to a glossy shine, the sofa, not antique but complementing the wooden coffee and end tables. "This room doesn't look much like you. But now that I know you used to live here, I understand the different style of the spare bedroom. It's not nearly as feminine as this room or the master bedroom."

"The room in the back right corner?" Matt asked.

Aubrey nodded. "It has its share of antiques, but they're more masculine." The signs on the walls were from old gas stations. The bed was an antique iron bed painted black.

He shook his head again. "You didn't have to keep all the decorations. As far as I'm concerned you can throw it all away. It's just a bunch of old junk."

Aubrey frowned. "I would never. I came to Whiskey Gulch with not much more than a couple of suitcases. I didn't have the money to purchase furniture or decorations. I was shocked to find a house so quickly that was fully furnished."

"Now you know the reason it was available."

"It didn't make a difference."

"And now?" He raised his eyebrows. "Now that you know there are some bad guys out there who could harm you?"

"I'm all the more determined to live here and bring those guys down." She clenched her fists. "No one should have to live in fear for her life."

"The problem with coyotes is that when you stop one, another takes his place. The money is too good to stop the trafficking."

"Then they'll have to take their business elsewhere," Aubrey said. "Whiskey Gulch is too nice a town to be held in fear by terrorists."

"You're willing to risk your life to make that happen?"

"Are you willing to turn a blind eye to the suffering of others?" Aubrey shot back. "What about that woman who died tonight? What if these coyotes were the ones who murdered your mother? Don't you want to see them brought to justice?" Aubrey pressed her balled fist to her chest, her eyes clouding with tears. "I wouldn't be able to live with myself if I did nothing to find that little girl. She deserves a better life than what those monsters have in store for her."

Matt stared at her for a long time. "You're very passionate about this."

"Damn right I am. We have to find her. Before it's too late. I can't let something horrible happen again." She turned away before the tears slipped down her cheeks. "I won't let it happen again."

Hands gripped her shoulders and turned her. "What do you mean, *again*?"

Aubrey's body trembled with the force of her grief. She couldn't speak past the massive lump in her throat.

He didn't push her for an answer. Instead, he waited for her to get a grip on her emotions.

How long did it take for the grief to mellow? Two years? Four? Ten? Aubrey swallowed hard and stared at Matt's chest, refusing to raise her face to his scrutiny. "My little girl would have turned six a month ago."

His fingers tightened. "You have a daughter?"

She shook her head, the tears slipping faster down her cheeks to drip off her chin. *"Had."* A sob rose up her throat. Aubrey struggled to tamp it back down. "She…she was taken…from our front yard." The guilt she'd felt for turning her back for that single, catastrophic minute threatened to consume her all over again. "She was taken. We looked for weeks. Her body was found by a farmer's dog in a field not far from where we lived."

Matt muttered a curse beneath his breath. "Did they find the man who took her?"

Aubrey shook her head. "No."

Matt's fingers tightened on her arms. "I'm sorry."

She shrugged. "It was two years ago, but it seems like yesterday. I'd give my life for her, if I could. Katie didn't even get to live hers. She was three years old. Three years."

Matt enveloped her in his arms and brought her gently against his chest.

Aubrey leaned her cheek on the hard expanse of muscles and listened to the beat of the man's heart. The sound gave her a strange sense of hope. Though she'd lost her baby girl, others still lived and breathed around her.

At one point after they'd found Katie's small body, Aubrey had wanted to die in order to be with her little girl. She worried that Katie was alone and afraid, missing her mama. The pain had been so intense, breathing had been a chore. Her depression had been so deep, she hadn't seen what it was doing to her marriage. Her husband blamed her for their daughter's death. She should have kept Katie close, never taking her eye off the child.

"One minute," Aubrey whispered into Matt's shirt.

"One minute?" he asked, tipping her chin up so that he could look into her eyes. "What do you mean?"

"One minute was all it took for my child to disappear. One minute that changed my life forever." She met his gaze through the tears swimming in her eyes. "I can't save Katie, but I will not let Isabella die without giving it my all to save her."

MATT HELD AUBREY in his arms, starring down into her watery green eyes, wishing he could take away this woman's pain. "You aren't responsible for Isabella," he reminded her. "Let the sheriff and his people find her."

"What if they don't? If I don't start looking now, it could be too late when the sheriff's department…" Her fingers dug into his shirt. "A child needs to be loved, not tortured. Katie… I should have been there for her."

Matt didn't know what to say to make Aubrey feel better. Having never had a child of his own, he could only imagine the pain of losing her. So he held her close, smoothing his hand over her hair until the sobs stopped shaking her body and her tears dried.

Eventually, she pushed against his chest. "I'm sorry. I made your shirt wet. If you like, I can put it through the wash."

Her eyes were red rimmed, and her face was streaked with the tracks of her tears. Still, she was beautiful with her auburn hair in disarray from her flight through the woods and the ride on the back of the motorcycle.

"I'd been doing so well. I haven't had a tearfest in six months." Her mouth twisted. "Crying is a waste of time and emotion. With anger, at least I get things done."

"Like what?"

"I throw myself into cleaning or working out. Crying saps my energy."

"Being shot at and running through the woods will sap your energy too. You need to rest." He tipped his head toward the room his mother used to sleep in. It was strange that someone else slept there now. But Aubrey was a gentle soul like his mother. It didn't feel so bad knowing she was the one living in his mother's house. His mother would have liked her.

"How can I sleep when there's a little girl out there, scared and maybe hurting?" She looked up at him.

"There won't be anyone we can question until daylight," he argued. "They can't study the ground and look for clues until the sun comes up. You might as well get some shut-eye."

She shook her head. "Damn them. Damn them all. I wish I'd had a gun when I went out there. They might not have killed Rosa. I might have stopped them from taking Isabella."

"You don't know that. They might have turned your gun on you," he said. "You could be the one on the way to the coroner instead of Rosa."

"At least then Rosa's girls might still have their mama alive."

"Or both you and Rosa would be dead, Marianna would have been taken along with Isabella and no one would have known about the children." He reached for her and gripped her arms. "You're alive for a reason. That reason was to save the baby and help the sheriff find the missing girl."

Aubrey sighed. "Maybe."

"Not maybe. Now, go get some sleep. We'll head out at dawn and see what we can do to help in the search."

As Aubrey headed toward her bedroom, she stopped and turned back toward Matt. "Have you considered… Do you think…" She hesitated and then blurted, "Do you think the same people who killed Rosa killed your mother?"

The thought had crossed his mind. "It's been four years since my mother was killed. I doubt the same coyotes are still working the same area. And we don't know why she was killed or why she was out in that field."

"But it could have been. Or people like the ones who killed Rosa." Her gaze met his. "I'm sorry. I don't mean to bring up bad memories for you. But if we find the people who killed Rosa, maybe they know who killed your mother. If so, you might get closure."

"They never found the man who killed your daughter?" Matt asked.

Aubrey shook her head. "No." She bit down hard on her bottom lip; tears welled in her eyes. "I hate the thought that he's still out there and some other little girls could be his next victim. Katie would have died in vain."

Matt couldn't stand the torture in Aubrey's face. He crossed the room and pulled her into his arms again. "Look, we'll find the men who killed Rosa. And when we do, we'll see if they know anything about my mother's murder. I know a little about what you're going through. I wasn't here when my mother was killed. I feel like I should have been. At the very least, I should have been able to find her killer."

"It's hard to move on when things are left undone," she said into his shirt. "Some people never get over it."

"Is that what happened to Katie's father?" he asked.

Aubrey nodded. "And me. I never got over losing Katie. We were two broken people who couldn't put each other back together again. So, I saved him the hassle and left." She nodded toward a large envelope on the table. "My divorce was final last week. That's the decree, all signed, sealed and delivered. Our life as a family is officially over. Emotionally, it was over the day Katie was taken."

"Damn." Matt's heart squeezed hard in his chest. "What a lousy way to end a day. If it makes you feel better, why don't you hang out with me on the couch. We can put on an old movie and wait together for the sun to rise." He tipped her chin up. "Sound better?"

She nodded, the hint of a smile nudging the corners of her lips. "I couldn't sleep even if I wanted to."

"Okay, then. Do you have the makings for cocoa or tea?" he asked.

She nodded. "In the cabinet over the stove."

He smiled. "That's where my mother kept stuff like that."

"Let me get you something."

"No, I'm not the one who ran through the woods beating up terrorists." He guided her over to the sofa and eased her down. "Sit."

Aubrey frowned. "I'm not a dog."

"You're right. A dog would have ignored me with that command." He winked. "Tea or cocoa?"

"Cocoa," she said. "It's summer and it's warm outside, but something about cocoa is soothing and reminds me of a simpler time when my parents shouldered all my worries."

"Cocoa it is." He went to the kitchen he'd spent much of his young life in with his mother making dinner while he set the table for just the two of them. She'd never dated or brought a gentleman home. It had been just him and her up until the day he left to join the Marine Corps. Now that he thought back, she'd smiled and seen him off, but she'd been alone after he'd gone. No one to look out for her.

Guilt gnawed at Matt. He'd been so ready to shake the dust of Whiskey Gulch off his boots and get away from the small town and small-minded people he'd gone to school with. And yet, here he was, back in the town he swore he'd never return to. His mother was gone. Before he'd learned of his inheritance, he had no real reason to stay. But he had.

"You doing okay in there?" Aubrey appeared at the bar. "Need a hand?"

"I'm doing okay." He'd been standing in front of the stove, staring at the cabinets, unmoving.

"I'll get the cups," she said, and entered the small kitchen. "I keep them near the sink." Aubrey reached up into the cabinet and retrieved two mugs and set them on the counter.

"Again, that's where my mother kept them." He stared at the mug with the San Antonio skyline on it. "She always drank her coffee in the morning with that one."

"I saw no need to move or replace anything. I came with nothing from my marriage. I was very happy to find your mother's home, fully equipped." She frowned. "Does it bother you that I'm using her things?"

"Not at all. I think she would have been happy that someone who needed them is using them." He scooped cocoa mix from the container into the mug, his arm brushing against hers. "I think she would have liked you."

"She had an eye for beautiful old things most people would have thrown away."

"Yes, she did. And she breathed new life into them."

Aubrey nodded with a faint smile. "I think I would have liked her too."

He had the urge to pull her into his arms again and brush his lips across hers. A woman he'd only just met. What was wrong with him? "Milk or water?" he asked, moving away.

"Milk. I'll get it." She turned too quickly and ran into his chest. "Oh."

Matt reached out to capture her arms and steady her, holding her longer than was necessary. For some reason, he couldn't make himself let go.

She stared up at him. "Sorry."

"Not your fault." He did let go and stepped out of her way.

Aubrey retrieved the milk, poured it into the two cups and set them into the microwave on the counter. Soon, they were sitting on the couch, sipping the cocoa.

Matt had turned the lights off in the kitchen and dimmed the ones in the living room like he had so many times in his childhood. Everything about the night was strange, but right. He felt as if by being there for Aubrey, he somehow was making up for the fact he hadn't been there for his mother. It was stupid, but he couldn't shake the feeling he was supposed to be there at that moment.

With the cocoa consumed, Aubrey curled her feet up beneath her and laid her head on the couch cushion.

"You should sleep. I'll keep an eye on things while you do."

"I'm not sleepy," she said, followed by a huge yawn.

"Of course you're not." He took the cup from her hands and set it onto the table. Then he grabbed a throw blanket from the back of one of his mother's chairs and laid it across Aubrey.

"Thank you," she said. "For staying with me, when you have a bed waiting for you back at the ranch."

"No problem." He gathered their mugs and carried them into the kitchen, running water through them before putting them into the dishwasher.

"Matt," Aubrey called out. "Shh."

He shut off the water. "What?"

"Do you hear that?" She was sitting up straight, her head tilted slightly.

"Hear what?" he said, coming around the bar to stand in the living room. That's when he heard the sound of engines. Several engines, racing toward the house. Bright lights shone through the curtains into the house.

"Get on the floor!" he called out, reaching for the handgun he'd brought with him. He grabbed his cell phone and tossed it to her. "Call 911." He ran toward the light switches on the wall.

"Where are you going?" she asked.

He hit the levers, sending the room into shadowy darkness, and continued toward the windows. "I need to see what's going on out there."

"No. You need to get down."

"We have to know what's going on out there." Hunkering low, he ran toward the front of the house, where the noise was loudest.

Easing up to the side of the big picture window, he lifted the curtain, carefully, so as not to draw attention to him.

His blood ran cold. Outside were four ATVs lined up, the riders pointing semiautomatic weapons at the house. He dropped down, flattening himself to the floor. "I count four bogeys, heavily armed. Stay down. It's about to get ugly in here."

Before the last word came out of his mouth, they opened fire, raining bullets into the house.

Glass shattered, wood splintered and the quiet little cottage at the edge of town turned into a war zone.

Chapter Five

"Hello? Can you hear me?" Aubrey cried over the noise of gunfire and the house being barraged with bullets.

"You've reached 911. State your emergency."

"Bullets are flying everywhere. We need help. Now!" she shouted.

"Address?" the 911 operator asked.

Aubrey gave it and followed with, "Please send someone soon."

"Can you get to somewhere safe?" the operator asked.

"No. We're in the house, they're shooting non-stop. I'm afraid to move off the floor."

"We have a unit on the way as we speak."

"Better be more than one unit. There are four of them and it sounds like they have machine guns."

"Roger. Sending multiple units. Hold tight, help's on its way."

Matt crawled across the floor toward her. "Get

behind the sofa." He snagged one of the over-stuffed chairs and dragged it toward the back of the couch. "These might not stop a bullet, but they could slow it down."

He had her get behind the couch, then he pulled the chair around for even more protection. When he moved away from the improvised bunker, Aubrey grabbed his arm. "Where are you going?"

"I'm going to see if I can get a bead on one of the shooters. When the sheriff's deputies arrive those guys will disappear in all directions. We need one of them to tell us where they're keeping the girl."

"Damn it, Matt. They're showering us with bullets. The odds are you'll be hit."

He shot her a grin. "I was trained for combat as part of the Marine Force Reconnaissance. I know how to keep my head down. Stay here and stay low."

"Please," she said. "Stay with me."

"I need to do this."

"Matt, I'd hate to think of losing another person to those bastards." A bullet ripped through the back of the couch, just above Aubrey's head. She shrank lower.

"Oh, and here I was thinking you cared about me."

"I do!" she yelled, knowing she wouldn't talk

him out of taking a shot at the men pelting them with lead. "Geez! Won't they run out of ammunition soon?" Another bullet hit an inch lower than the last one.

"Not if they came with a bunch of spare magazines." He rolled to the side and low-crawled his way up toward the front window.

Aubrey peered around the edge of the sofa, her head low to the floor to keep from catching a bullet. She held her breath as Matt used his handgun to lift the curtain.

More bullets blasted through the broken glass, spraying shards across the floor.

Matt shook his head and crawled low to the ground, away from the window toward the hallway and the door leading to the front bedroom.

When he disappeared out of sight, Aubrey's heart beat so fast she thought she would pass out.

In the distance, the sound of sirens brought hope for a quick end to the onslaught.

Suddenly the gunfire ceased, engines revved and moved away from the house.

A loud bang sounded from the vicinity of the back bedroom.

Aubrey gasped.

Had one of the attackers come up to the bedroom and shot Matt?

She abandoned the cover of the sofa and chair and crawled on her hands and knees toward the hallway to the bedroom. "Matt?" she cried. Grabbing a lamp from the table in the hallway, she yanked the cord out of the wall, pushed to her feet and ran the rest of the way to the spare bedroom with the gas station signs on the wall. Raising the lamp high, she prepared to bash in the head of any coyote attacking Matt.

A man emerged from the room, straightening as he entered the hallway. He caught the lamp before it crashed into his head. As he did, his face came into view in the moonlight shining from the living room.

Matt.

"Please tell me you weren't going to use this on me," he said, setting the lamp on the table in the hall.

She flung herself into his arms. "Oh, thank God. You're alive."

"Of course, I'm alive." He grinned. "And the cavalry has arrived. But I need you to stay inside until I give you the all clear. I think I hit one of them."

"Let the sheriff's deputies get him," she said.

"I can't risk him getting away." Matt kept moving toward the door.

"But what if he's still conscious?" Aubrey ran after him. "He could still have his gun and shoot you."

"I'll be careful," he said. "But I can't have you

following me out there. I'll be too worried about you to keep my focus." He gripped her arms before they left the cover of the hallway and reentered the living room. "Do you understand? I need to know you're safe."

She nodded. "Okay, I'll stay here. But don't get shot."

"I'll do my best." He bent and brushed his lips across hers. "And you do the same. Stay here in the hallway. There are several walls between you and the bullets they could shoot."

Her lips tingled where he'd brushed his across them. That brief kiss had scrambled the thoughts in her head. Somehow in that one meeting of the lips, they'd crossed the line from strangers to something more.

Aubrey hunkered low in the hallway, her fingers pressed to her lips, her thoughts with the man heading out of the house where, a moment ago, four armed criminals had turned their weapons on the home Matt had grown up in. Not because of him, but because of her attack on them.

The men were ruthless. If one of them was lying on the ground wounded, he wouldn't hesitate to shoot Matt.

Hovering on the edge of staying safe and wanting to go out and do what she could to protect the man who'd saved her life, Aubrey forced herself to remain in place.

Sirens wailed, moving closer to Maple Street and the little cottage on the edge of town.

"Please hurry," she murmured.

As if hearing her quiet entreaty, the wailing grew louder until it echoed off the exterior walls of the house. Lights shone through the broken windows, giving the shattered interior of the living room an eerie glow.

Unable to stay in place a moment longer, Aubrey emerged from the hallway and moved to the front door. Rays of light shone through the bullet holes into the room, creating a spectacle like something out of a laser tag game room. She had the urge to duck beneath the tiny beams to get to the door. When she reached for the doorknob, she hesitated.

"Aubrey," Matt's voice called out. "All clear. You can come out."

She yanked open the door and shaded her eyes against the glare of the headlights. "Matt?"

"Over here," he said.

She followed the sound of his voice. The people moving about the front yard were nothing more than silhouettes against the light from the four sheriff's vehicles. Another siren wailed nearby. Soon an ambulance pulled up behind the sheriff's vehicles and the EMTs jumped out.

"Aubrey," Matt said.

She followed Matt's voice to where he knelt

beside a man lying on the ground next to a four-wheeler. Sheriff Richards stood over him. Matt had his hand pressed to a wound in the man's chest.

Anger burned in Aubrey's heart. This could be the man who'd killed Rosa. If they didn't need him alive to tell them where they'd taken Isabella, Aubrey would be tempted to shove a knife in his wound and twist.

"Do you speak Spanish?" the sheriff asked.

Aubrey clenched her fists and nodded. "A little."

"See if you can understand what he's saying," Sheriff Richards said. "I know very few words."

Kneeling beside the injured man, Aubrey leaned close to hear the words he was saying in a gurgling whisper. "*Destruir la casa de los ángeles.*" He repeated the words over and over as blood dripped out of the side of his mouth.

"Do you understand what he's saying?" Matt asked.

Aubrey focused on the broken words from the injured man, making the translation in her head. "I think he's saying *destroy the house of angels*." She had a hard time feeling sorry for the man lying on the ground, bleeding out. He, or one of his cohorts, had killed Rosa, a mother of two, and stolen Isabella. Aubrey wanted to shake him, to yell at him and force him to tell her where they'd taken Isabella.

"Didn't Rosa call the cottage the house of angels?" Matt asked.

In Spanish, Aubrey asked, *"Donde está la chica?"* Where is the girl?

"La tienen," he said, and coughed spittle and blood. His head fell back, and his eyes closed.

Aubrey's heart leaped. This guy couldn't die. Not until he told them where they could find the child. *"Donde?"* She grabbed his shoulders and shook the man. *"Donde está la chica?"*

The emergency medical technicians arrived at her side and set their tool kits and the backboard on the ground.

Matt wrapped his hands around Aubrey's shoulders. "Let the EMTs do their job. Maybe they can save him or revive him long enough to answer a few questions."

Aubrey struggled to break free of his grip. "He has to know where they took the girl. He has to know."

"He's not going to tell you as long as he's unconscious," Matt said. "Let the techs do what they can to keep him alive."

Aubrey let Matt draw her to her feet. She was shaking, not from shock or fear, but from rage. "The bastard doesn't deserve to live. But he better not die before we get the information we need out of him."

The EMTs worked over the man, applying pressure to his wound and attempting to stabilize him before transport to a medical facility.

Matt stood with Aubrey, watching them load him into the ambulance and drive away.

Sheriff Richards turned back to the cottage. "I'm sorry about the house," he said. "If I had any clue they'd attack you, I'd have sent a unit by to camp out in your driveway. "You two are okay? No injuries?"

"I'm fine." Matt looked Aubrey over from head to toe. "Are you?"

Her gaze on the disappearing ambulance, Aubrey nodded. "As well as to be expected after having the house I live in destroyed." Her brow furrowed and she faced Matt. "I'm so sorry. This was your home. The house your mother lived in. They destroyed it."

Matt took her hands in his. "Nothing a few new windows, boards and paint won't fix."

Aubrey glanced at the many bullet holes in the siding and snorted. "You're kidding, right? It'll take a lot more than that to set this house to rights."

He pulled her into his arms and rested his chin on her hair. "I'm just glad you're not hurt."

Aubrey let the tension ease out of her. When

Matt wrapped his arms around her, she believed everything would be all right. "I'm glad you weren't hurt. You took some chances."

"None I wasn't fully aware of," he assured her.

The sheriff walked toward the house. "Can you think of a reason why they'd call your mother's cottage the house of angels?"

Matt loosened his hold on Aubrey and shrugged. "My mother was a good person, but she wasn't a saint. And she's been gone for four years. I'm not sure what that's all about, but I know someone who might."

"You do?" Aubrey asked. "Who?"

"One of my used parts suppliers. Juan Salazar. He knows everyone in the county." Matt grinned. "Maybe even everyone in South Texas. The man gets around and salvages parts from junkyards and sells them to me. When I have a customer who can't afford the price of new parts, he finds the part and brings it to me at a discounted price."

"I know the guy," the sheriff said. "Do you want me to bring him in for questioning?"

Matt shook his head. "No. He might get skittish. I'm not quite certain of his immigration status. He might only talk to me since we've done business together."

The sheriff nodded. "If you need backup, let me know."

"Will do," Matt said.

"In the meantime, Ms. Blanchard—" the sheriff frowned "—do you have a place to stay?"

Aubrey stared at the house, her heart mourning it. "This place gave me a new start. I hate to abandon it."

Matt was already shaking his head. "Ms. Blanchard will be staying out at the Whiskey Gulch Ranch until further notice." He held up a hand when Aubrey opened her mouth to protest. "No argument. I can't leave you here, and you can't stay with anyone else. The ranch has security set up and enough armed men to provide you the protection you need."

The sheriff nodded. "That Travis boy—and you, Hennessey—are prior military. They know what to do."

"And if you try to stay anywhere else, you put those places at risk. They tried to get to you once," Matt said. "They will likely try again. Now they'll want me as well, since I shot one of their own. Best to keep the targets under one roof."

He had a good point.

Another glance at the cottage helped Aubrey make up her mind. "Okay. I'll go to the ranch. But I want to be there when you talk to Mr. Salazar."

Matt frowned. "He might not talk to me if he thinks we're ganging up on him."

"He might not object if you tell him she's your girlfriend," the sheriff said.

Aubrey's heart fluttered. Matt's girlfriend.

Sheriff Richards frowned. "Unless you have a girlfriend he already knows about."

Matt's gaze met Aubrey's. "I don't have a girlfriend. He might open up if I tell him Aubrey's my girlfriend. But he wouldn't be as forthcoming with information if the sheriff's department comes with me."

The sheriff held up his hands. "I'll leave it to you. When do you think you can get hold of him?"

"As a matter of fact, he's bringing me a part today. I'll just ask him to come earlier. It's five o'clock now." He pulled out his phone and keyed in a text and waited. The cell phone chimed. Matt looked up. "He'll be by around seven."

"Good," Aubrey said.

"Do you want to go out to the ranch until then?" Matt asked. "You could clean up after the disaster they made of the cottage." He plucked a dust ball out of her hair. "Not that you look bad or anything."

Aubrey touched a hand to her hair. She probably looked awful. But how she looked didn't matter as much as a little girl being held captive or sold into the sex trade. "No. I don't want to go too far. We could get breakfast at the diner.

They open early. Then we can meet Salazar at your shop at seven." Aubrey's brow furrowed. "You don't think those men will shoot up the diner between now and then, do you?"

"My deputies congregate around the diner between five and seven, before shift change and after." Sheriff Richards patted his belly. "There will be uniforms and service vehicles around the place. I'd grab a bite myself, but my wife has me on a strict diet since my blood pressure is up."

"Breakfast sounds good. Maybe some of the locals will know more about the house of angels." Matt nodded toward the house. "Want to grab some of your things before we go? Then we won't have to come back later. We can go straight to the ranch."

Aubrey nodded. "Makes sense."

"Need help?"

"No. I'll be okay." Aubrey forced a smile, squared her shoulders and walked back into the house. She flipped the switch on the wall, illuminating the damage, and her heart sank into the pit of her belly. All of Lynn Hennessey's beautiful antique furniture lay in shambles.

Just when she'd thought she was well on her way to establishing herself in her new life, Aubrey was back to square one. In need of a place to call home. That overwhelming feeling of hopelessness washed over her.

Starting over was so hard. Tears welled in her eyes. And there was a little girl out there in a worse place than she was. How was she going to find her and bring her to safety?

Hands came up to rest on her shoulders. "They're just things," Matt said. "Things can be replaced."

"I know. But they were your mother's things. And your mother is gone."

"She's gone, but my memories of her are very much alive and a part of me." He turned her around and pulled her into his arms. "The important thing to remember now is that you're alive." His gaze left her face and scanned the room, his lips firming. "If you look around you, you'll realize how easily this could have ended much worse."

She nodded, her gaze following his, her heart fluttering. "You're right. This could have ended differently. Aubrey squared her shoulders. "I have to believe we survived this for a reason."

"And that reason is a little girl who needs our help." Matt brushed the hair back from her forehead. "Come on, let's get you packed."

"How much should I bring?" she asked.

"How much do you have?"

"Not a whole lot."

"Then let's pack it all. Until the windows are

replaced or boarded, anyone could walk in and take what they want."

Aubrey frowned. "Should we stick around and board the windows?"

"I'm not worried about it. We have to find Isabella. We can take care of the house after we find her."

Aubrey nodded. "It won't take long."

"Let me help." He followed her into his mother's bedroom. "Where do you keep your suitcases?"

"In the back of the closet," she said.

Matt opened the closet door, pulled out the suitcases she'd stored there and opened them on the bed. "Do you want me to pack the hanging clothes?"

Aubrey hesitated for a moment. The thought of Matt's hands on her clothes sent a ripple of awareness through her. She drew in a deep breath and tried to relax. They were just clothes. "Yes. Please." She'd liked the way it felt when he'd touched her arms or put his arm around her waist or shoulders. He was solid and safe. But more than that, he was so male and sexy.

Aubrey focused on emptying the dresser, one drawer at a time, hurrying to hide the lace panties she'd bought after her divorce as a subversive act of rebellion. Her ex would never see her in those panties. She tucked them beneath some

T-shirts while casting a surreptitious glance toward Matt, wondering what his reaction would be if he saw her wearing the lacy panties.

He had dumped a pile of her clothes into the suitcase and gone back to the closet for more. "I can't believe I'd forgotten about this." Matt shoved aside several dresses on a hanger and stared at the wall in the back of the closet.

Aubrey had always loved that the closet was lined with cedar paneling.

"Forgotten what?" Aubrey's eyes narrowed and she moved to join him at the open doors. "Did the bullets damage this room as well?"

"No." He leaned in and pressed against one of the panels. A small door sprang open and a light blinked on. The door was just big enough for Matt to squeeze through as he turned sideways and slipped inside. Then he disappeared and the door closed automatically behind him.

Aubrey gasped, her heart pounding. "Matt?"

Chapter Six

Matt descended the narrow metal staircase into a concrete bunker no bigger than eight by ten feet. One wall was lined with shallow shelves filled with canned goods and pantry staples. At the end of the room were several army cots folded neatly. Beside them was a larger shelf filled with blankets, clothing and shoes in a variety of sizes.

Matt studied the supplies, his heart swelling. He knew now why they'd called this the house of angels.

The secret panel above opened and Aubrey called out, "Matt?"

"Come down," he said. "I think this might explain some things."

Her footsteps sounded on the metal treads as she descended into the bunker. "Oh, my, what is this place?"

Matt shook his head. "I'd forgotten about this old storm shelter. On a few rare occasions when my mother came down to clean, I'd play in here as a kid. As I grew older, I didn't hang out at the house much. I completely forgot about this space."

"Apparently, your mother didn't." Aubrey ran her fingers along the rows of canned goods. "She had this place fully stocked. Was she expecting Armageddon?"

Matt stared across the small space at Aubrey and held up clothes and shoes that could only fit a small child. A girl. Nothing a younger version of Matt would have worn. "I think she was hiding people in the shelter."

Aubrey's eyes widened. *"La casa de los ángeles."*

"The house of angels." Matt laid the clothing and shoes back on the shelf.

"This cottage must have been a haven for the people trying to escape human trafficking."

Matt ran a hand through his hair. "Mom, what were you doing?"

"You didn't know about any of this, did you?"

He shook his head. "I joined the Marine Corps right after high school. I'd been gone with only a few holiday and birthday visits in the eleven years I was on active duty. She never said a word."

"And if she had, what would you have done?" Aubrey asked, her voice soft and warm.

Matt shot a frown her way. "Stopped her."

"Imagine the people whose lives she saved," Aubrey said. "Where would they be now?"

"I don't know. If my mother hadn't gotten into the business of rescuing lost causes, she might be alive today."

"You don't know that."

"Why couldn't she be like normal mothers and stick to gossip and baking cookies?"

Aubrey laughed. "Now, that's a sexist thing to say. Most mothers I know are working full-time, raising children and taking care of a household. They wear multiple hats and still manage to make their families happy and stay sane."

Matt sighed. "Sorry." He looked around again. "My mother never played by society's rules. She worked at the feedstore instead of taking a job as a secretary or office staff. She liked helping customers find the right vitamin supplements for their ailing livestock, or the best tools to use to trim a horse's hooves. She grew up on a farm, but she dressed and acted the lady always, even in the male-centric environment of the feedstore. She was a single mother, raising a boy on her own. She didn't want me to grow up to be lazy or unable to defend myself. She insisted I get a job while I was in school, and she made me take self-defense classes when other kids bullied me. I guess that's when I established myself as a badass with attitude. No one bothered me after that."

"She must have been an amazing woman."

Matt nodded, his heart hurting. "She was. And I didn't spend nearly enough time with her. If I could do it over…"

"I bet she wouldn't have had it any other way. She probably knew you needed to get out of Whiskey Gulch, and that the Marine Corps was the place where you could build a career and prove yourself."

"Prove myself to whom?" His gaze captured hers. "By then, I didn't give a damn what the people of Whiskey Gulch thought about me."

Aubrey touched his arm. "Perhaps you needed to prove yourself to you."

He covered her hand with his. "The point is, I should have known what was going on here. I might have been able to keep her safe."

"From the other side of the world? You were in the Marine Corps," Aubrey said. "What could you have done?"

"I could have gotten out and come back to be with her. She might have been doing what she was doing out of loneliness."

"I doubt that's why she did it," Aubrey said. "She probably just wanted to help those who were being preyed upon."

"Well, we're not helping Isabella by standing

in a storm shelter. Let's get out of here, have breakfast and find Juan. Maybe he knows something about my mother's secret activities." He balled his fist. "It galls me to think that strangers knew about my mother's activities, and I didn't."

He waved toward the stairs. "Do you want to go first, or do you want me to?"

"I'll go." She spun toward the stairs and started up.

After another glance around, Matt followed.

When she reached the top, Aubrey pushed on the panel. It opened outward with a gentle swish. "I can't believe I've been here for two months and this is the first I've noticed the panel in the back of my closet." She stepped out into the bedroom and waited for Matt.

Matt exited the hidden storm shelter, turned and watched as the door closed automatically. "It blends in well with the surrounding cedar paneling. My mother told me it was here when she moved in. Whoever lived here before she bought the place was afraid of tornadoes and had the storm shelter built into the house."

"It's made like one of those cold war bunkers you read about. I imagine it would withstand the harshest tornado."

Matt finished loading her clothing, hangers and all, into her suitcase and threw in several pairs of shoes. When the case was past full, he closed it and leaned down on the bulging mass to drag the zipper around.

Aubrey was just zipping her own suitcase. "I'll grab the stuff from the bathroom." She hurried into the bathroom and scooped toiletries into a large bag she'd retrieved from the closet shelf.

While she was in the other room, Matt looked around the bedroom. At the back of the house, it was relatively untouched by the war the attackers had waged on the front of the dwelling. Most of the decorations were what his mother had left behind. A single photograph stood on the nightstand.

Matt lifted it and stared into Aubrey's beautiful, happy face. She held a little girl with strawberry blond hair and green eyes so much like Aubrey's, it had to be her child.

Aubrey emerged from the bathroom with a sigh. The circles beneath her eyes were indicative of the sleepless night she'd had. "I think that's all. The rest was here when I arrived." When she saw what he held in his hand, she paused, drew in a deep breath and let it out slowly.

"She looks so much like you," he said.

Aubrey nodded. "Everyone said she was a miniature version of me." She held out her hand.

Matt placed the photograph in her palm, his knuckles brushing against her skin. A shock of electricity passed up his arm and spread throughout his body, warming him all over.

Aubrey's pupils flared briefly, before her gaze dropped to the image of herself and her daughter.

"She's beautiful," Matt said. What else could he say?

Aubrey nodded. "She was a happy child, always singing and dancing around the house. When she disappeared...all the light left our home."

"I can't say that I know how it feels to lose a child, but it must have been hard."

A single tear slipped from Aubrey's eye and dropped onto the glass cover of the picture frame. She reached out to wipe it away. Then she looked up, her lips pressing into a firm line. "I'm ready."

Matt could tell she was holding herself together by a thin thread. Dwelling on her loss wouldn't change the outcome for Katie. Moving on might change the outcome for Isabella. "Let's go."

He led the way from the house and to the shed out back where he'd parked his motorcycle beside her Jeep earlier that morning. The shed had several bullet holes in it but wasn't nearly as damaged as the exterior of the front of the house.

"I'd like to take my Jeep," Aubrey said. "I'm almost afraid if I leave it here, those killers might come back and trash it like they trashed the house."

Matt nodded. "Okay. How about you follow me to my shop? You know where that is?"

"On Main Street?" she asked.

"That's it." He rocked the motorcycle off the stand. "I'll lock up my motorcycle at my shop and we can go to the diner in your Jeep."

She smiled. "I like that plan."

His heart warmed at her smile. She needed to smile more. If he had any say in the matter, he would see to it she had more reasons to smile. Losing a child had to leave a permanent hole in her heart. He hurt for her.

Matt rolled his bike out of the shed and waited for Aubrey to back out her Jeep. After he'd closed the shed door, he took off for his shop with Aubrey following. Once there, he locked up his bike before joining Aubrey out front.

She stood beside her Jeep. "Do you want to drive?"

"Only if you want me to," he said.

"If it's all the same to you, I'd like to drive. It might be the only thing I have in my control right now."

"By all means. It leaves my trigger finger free, should I need to fire my gun."

Her lips pinched. "I hope we don't have a need for it anytime soon."

"You and me both. Since I got out of the Marine Corps, I thought I wouldn't need to shoot at another individual, that I'd only use my handgun to shoot at rattlesnakes and wild boar." He shook his head. "I didn't realize just how many bad guys resided on US soil."

"Makes you wonder what the world is coming to." Aubrey climbed into the driver's seat.

Matt settled in the passenger seat and secured his safety belt.

With Aubrey driving, he had a chance to study her in the gray light of early morning.

"How long have you been in Whiskey Gulch?" he asked.

"Two months."

"I'd seen you around, but I hadn't realized you'd moved into my mother's old house."

"Do you still own the house?" she asked.

"I do. I use a leasing agency to rent it and let them handle the details. But I haven't been inside it since my mother was murdered. I just couldn't bring myself to go inside the house I grew up in. She wouldn't be there. It wouldn't be the same."

Aubrey shot a glance his way. "I'm sorry. I didn't know it would be that painful."

"Actually, it wasn't. You made it better."

She smiled, the gesture fading immediately. "And now it's destroyed."

He shook his head. "It can be fixed. Besides, it was about time to do some remodeling."

Her brow furrowed. "But your mother's things…"

"They're just things," he said.

"You don't want to keep anything?"

"I'll probably keep a couple of the things she treasured most, but that's it."

Aubrey nodded. "Will you still rent it out? Or are you moving in?"

Matt stared across the console at Aubrey. "You're welcome to live there as long as you like. Although, after what happened a few hours ago, I doubt you'd want to go back there."

She shivered. "I'm not sure now whether they were after me, or there to destroy the house of angels."

"It could have been a combination of both. If they are the ones responsible for my mother's death, they might have decided killing her wasn't enough to stop people from seeking sanctuary in the house of angels."

Aubrey pulled into the parking lot at the diner and shifted into Park. "So, they wanted to destroy the house with me in it to deter anyone else from picking up the torch?"

"I can't say for sure, but we need to treat the attack as something along those lines." He got out, went around to the driver's side and held the door open for her. "You aren't safe living alone, as long as those people are still free and armed."

MATT HELD OUT his hand and Aubrey grasped it and let him help her out of the vehicle. "I can't take advantage of others." With him so close and his hand holding hers, she felt secure and hyper-aware all at once.

"You can. And you will." He didn't release her hand, nor did he move out of her way. "If staying at the ranch is bothering you, I'd invite you to stay at my apartment over my shop. The problem with that is that it's too exposed and you'd have the same issue as you did at my mother's cottage."

She squeezed his hand, her chest tightening. "I don't want what happened to your mother's house to happen to your shop or apartment."

He brought her hand up to his chest. "At the ranch, there's more security available and more people who can protect you."

"And more people I'd put in harm's way if those men are determined to make me pay for attacking them and taking the baby they might have counted on selling for big bucks." Her jaw hardened. "We have to find Marianna's sister."

"And if, in the process, we discover where the coyotes are hiding," Matt's jaw hardened, "we'll put them out of everyone's misery."

Still holding his hand, Aubrey's fingers tightened around his. "I like the way you think."

They entered the diner, hand in hand and found a booth near the back, sitting side by side with their backs against the wall.

Aubrey chuckled. "Now I understand why gangsters and gamblers sit like this. I have to be able to see what's coming."

"Sadly true," Matt agreed.

As Aubrey studied the people in the room, a man entered the diner, dressed in a suit. He paused at the door, his gaze taking in all the occupants of the room. When he got to Aubrey and Matt, his eyes narrowed slightly. Then he smiled and strode toward them.

"Do you know that man walking our way?" Aubrey asked.

"That's Mr. Morrison." His lips thinned. "He hit on my mother back when I was in high school. Asked her to go out with him a couple of times. I remember my mother giving him one excuse after another as to why she couldn't. The man didn't like to take no for an answer."

"Matthew Hennessey." Morrison stuck out his hand as he neared their table.

Matt stayed in his seat but took the man's hand and shook it briefly. "Morrison."

"And this is?" Morrison smiled at Aubrey.

She gave him her name, and without missing

a beat, he said, "Ms. Blanchard, let me know if you want to invest in a home of your own. I have a few very nice listings you might be interested in. Just came on the market this week."

"Thank you, Mr. Morrison, but I'm not ready for that kind of commitment, yet."

"Well, keep me in mind when you are." He turned his attention back to Matt. "And with your inheritance, Matthew, you might want to consider converting cash into assets. You have the one rental property. Why not add a couple to generate more passive income?"

"Thank you, but I have enough assets to manage now."

Morrison pulled a couple of business cards out of his front pocket and laid them on the table in front of each of them. "When you're ready, give a call."

"Thank you," Aubrey said. "Right now, all I want is a very large coffee."

The Realtor moved on to a table on the other end of the diner.

A middle-aged waitress stopped at the table, plunked two coffee mugs in front of them and poured steamy brew into each one. "Hi, Matt. You haven't been in for a couple of days. Who's your friend?"

Matt smiled at the waitress. "Hey, Barb. This

is Aubrey. Aubrey, meet Barb, the best waitress in Whiskey Gulch."

"I heard that," another waitress called out. "And what am I? Chopped liver?"

Matt chuckled. "I stand corrected. Barb and Dottie are two of the best waitresses in Whiskey Gulch."

"That's more like it," Dottie called out with a good-natured grin. "You treat that boy right, Barb."

"I've got this." Barb returned her attention to her table. "What can I get you two?"

They placed their orders for eggs, bacon and toast and sat back, sipping the hot coffee.

Aubrey sighed. "I needed this."

"You say you're a home health care nurse?" Matt asked.

"I am," Aubrey replied. "I need to check on a patient today."

"I'll go with you."

"That's not necessary."

"Sweetheart, you were nearly killed a few hours ago." He reached for her free hand and brought it to his lips. "I'm going with you." She didn't know if this tender gesture was part of his act as her boyfriend, but she liked it.

"Why you? Couldn't I get one of the sheriff's deputies to shadow me?"

Matt nodded. "But why do that, when you have me?"

"I don't want to—"

"Be a bother." Matt shook his head. "You're not a bother."

Though she enjoyed the way he was holding her hand and the touch of his lips on her knuckles, her frown deepened. "Will I put my patients at risk by going out to visit them?"

Matt tilted his head. "It's possible. Although, the attacks have all been under the cover of darkness. I think as long as you stick to daylight hours, they will be okay."

"Good, because Mrs. Blair is expecting me at noon to help her with her lunch and meds. She recently had hip replacement surgery and doesn't have anyone else to help." Aubrey thought about her workweek, coming to a conclusion she didn't like but knew was the right strategy. "I'm going to call the service and have one of the other nurses cover for me for the next few days. I want to focus on finding Isabella."

"That might work out for the best anyway. It will make it easier for us to keep an eye on you."

She twisted her lips. "Now you make it sound like I need a bodyguard."

"You do." He snorted softly. "The attack on the cottage should have convinced you of that."

Aubrey couldn't argue that. A flashback of the

terror she'd felt while being fired on nonstop for what felt like a lifetime reminded her of what she'd lived through. Because of Matt. "Okay. I guess I do need a bodyguard."

"And you're in luck." He sat back with a grin. "I'm free and volunteering for the task."

"Thank you."

He released her hand and set his coffee mug on the table. "Thank me when we come out the other side of this nightmare intact."

Barb brought their food and set it on the table in front of them. Her eyes narrowed. "What's this I heard about your old house getting shot up last night? You weren't in it, were you?"

Matt looked at Aubrey. "As a matter of fact, we were."

Barb's eyes widened. "Both of you?"

Aubrey nodded with Matt.

"Dear Lord, I'm glad you came out relatively unscathed." She looked at them closely. "You weren't injured, were you?" Her gaze took in Aubrey.

"Not really," Aubrey said. "Thanks to Matt. He knew what to do."

"I hear they took one of the guys who shot at you to the hospital in Kerrville," Barb continued. "Who were they and why did they shoot at your house?"

"We don't know for sure," Matt said. "You

seem to have heard a lot. Have you heard rumors about who they might be?"

Barb shot a glance around the diner and bent closer. "I heard there's one of those people brokers in the area. You know, the kind that sells little girls."

Aubrey leaned toward the woman. "Do you know where he might be located?"

Barb frowned. "Those guys aren't going to announce where they're holed up. I bet they move around a lot to keep from being caught. Whiskey Gulch might be a small town, but this is big country, with lots of places to hide." She shook her head. "No. I just heard they're in the area. Told my girlfriends with kids to keep them close. Crying shame we have to be so careful these days. Too many nutjobs out there." Barb frowned. "You don't have little ones, do you?"

Aubrey closed her eyes to the pain and drew in a deep breath, letting it out slowly.

Matt reached for Aubrey's hand and squeezed it.

"Did I say something wrong?" Barb asked.

Aubrey shook her head. "No. It's okay. I had a little girl. She's no longer with me."

"I'm sorry." Barb's lips pressed together. "There I go, putting my foot in my mouth."

"No, really. It's not your fault. I should be better at handling that question by now."

"No mother who has lost a child is ever going to handle the pain," Barb said. "I can imagine it never goes away." She paused, overcome with emotion. "I'm sorry for your loss. She must have been very special to have a mother who loved her as much as you did."

"She was special." Aubrey fought back the ready tears that surfaced when she spoke of Katie.

"You two eat while the food's hot." Barb turned away, rubbing her eye. "Got something in my eye I need to take care of."

Aubrey lifted her fork, determined to eat, despite the fact her appetite had gone.

"I'm sorry. Barb has a big heart."

"And a big mouth," Dottie called out.

"And there are no secrets in this town," Matt said loud enough that everyone in the diner could hear.

Aubrey laughed at the friendly exchange of barbs between the waitress and Matt. It spoke of familiarity and mutual respect, laced with sarcasm. "I take it you come here often."

Matt grinned at Dottie. "I had, until I inherited half of the Whiskey Gulch Ranch. Up until then, I ate breakfast here every other day."

"Every other day?"

"Yeah. I would have eaten here every day, but it got expensive tipping the waitresses." He winked at Barb as she passed him, carrying a carafe of coffee.

"We're worth it," Barb said.

"Every penny," Matt said. In a lower voice, he said, "Dottie and Barb were friends to my mother. I guess that's why I like it here so much. They remind me of her."

"Like you're closer to her by being here."

He nodded.

Aubrey leaned closer. "Did they know what she was doing in that storm shelter?"

Matt's eye narrowed. "Good question. Let's ask." He waved to Barb. "Could I get you to top off my coffee?"

Barb finished at her other table and hurried over with the carafe of hot coffee. "Do you need anything else?"

"Actually," Matt said, "I have a question for you and Dottie."

"Dottie, get your carcass over here. Our boy wants you."

"I haven't had a handsome man want me in I don't know how long." Dottie hurried over, tucking her notepad into the pocket of her apron. "What can I do for you?"

"You two were my mother's friends," Matt started. "Did you spend much time at the cottage?"

Dottie laughed. "*Did* we?"

"Thursday evening was our poker night," Barb said. "Phyllis, from the library, was our fourth." She sighed. "I miss those nights."

"Only because you won half the time." Dottie shook her head. "It was nice because we could walk there and walk home, after having a few glasses of wine or whiskey." Her eyes shadowed. "I miss those nights."

"I miss Lynn," Barb said, her shoulders drooping. "She was the nicest person you ever met. She'd do anything for anyone."

Matt shared a glance with Aubrey. "Did she share her secrets?"

Dottie turned to Barb. "She was tight-lipped. If we told her a secret, she kept it."

"What about her own secrets?" Aubrey asked.

Barb crossed her arms over her chest. "Like Dottie said, if she had a secret, she kept it. It blew our minds when we found out her only son was James Travis's firstborn. As far as I know, she was the only one who knew that secret. Even the lawyer didn't know what was in the letter he delivered to James. And then none of us knew until James was killed and the will was read."

"Talk about setting the town on fire with gossip." Dottie grinned. "We're just glad our favorite customer got some of what was coming to him."

"Yeah, you put up with a lot from those snot-nosed high school kids picking on you because you didn't have a father," Barb said.

"How did you know that?" Matt asked.

"Your mama told us how she put you in martial arts training and how that set those other kids straight," Dottie said.

Barb nodded. "None of us were surprised you joined the Marine Corps and got the hell out of this small-minded town." She turned to Aubrey. "We all knew he was destined for bigger and better things. His mama was so proud when he made it into Marine Force Reconnaissance. She was practically busting the buttons off her blouse all through our poker game that week. I beat the pants off her, she was so distracted and excited."

"We were surprised when you came back to stay after your mama died," Dottie said quietly.

"Other than the secret about my lineage, did she share anything else about her life that she might have wanted to keep secret from the rest of the town?" Matt asked.

Dottie frowned at Barb. "Not sure what you're talking about."

Barb shook her head. "If she didn't want anyone to know something…they didn't know. She was that good."

"Why?" Dottie's eyes widened. "Was she in witness protection or something like that?"

"I could see her being in witness protection,"

Barb said. "Other than the four of us having drinks once a week, she didn't spend time with too many others unless she was helping them at the feedstore."

Having sat back and observed Matt trying to lead the ladies into confessing to knowing something about Lynn Hennessey's storm shelter, Aubrey became impatient. "Did she have any secrets about the house she lived in?"

Dottie's eyes narrowed. "I feel like you're trying to lead us to the water, but we're not drinking. What are you trying to ask? Just go ahead and spit it out."

"Did you know there was a storm cellar in her house?" Matt asked.

Barb laughed. "Of course we did. That's where she went to get the wine."

"Did she take you down there?" Aubrey asked.

"No." Dottie waved a hand. "We were always deep in a game when she'd go down to get more to drink."

Barb tilted her head to the side. "Although one time, I swear she was talking to herself in her bedroom. In Spanish, no less." Barb grinned. "I had far too much whiskey that night."

"Why do you ask, Matt?" Dottie wanted to know. "Did you need to get rid of her stash of wine? We'll gladly take it off your hands. Not that we have poker games anymore. None of us had the heart to bring someone new into the game. It just wouldn't feel right. God broke the mold when he made Lynn. She was a pure joy to know and call my friend."

"That's the truth," Barb said. "Or did she have a body buried down there? We always wondered if she'd killed her husband and that was why she was raising her boy alone. It's those quiet ones you have to worry about."

"Oh, shush, Barb," Dottie said. "Lynn didn't have a mean bone in her body. If she had, she would have outed James Travis as Matt's father a long time ago."

"You have a point," Barb said. "Is there anything else you want to know about your dear mother?"

"No. I think that about covers it. Thank you, ladies," Matt said. "Now, if you could bring me my bill, I might consider leaving a tip." When they turned to go, he stopped them, "Ladies..."

Both women turned back to face him.

"Thank you for being a friend to my mother. I know how much she treasured her time with you. She'd send me letters about getting together with her friends. Had I known she was playing poker, I would have sent her some stake money."

"Oh, we played for pennies and sometimes baked goods," Barb said. "It was never about the money. Some of our dreams were out there, I'm tellin' you. Someone wanted to be a war correspondent, and another wanted to be a pole dancer at a gentleman's club."

"That was me." Dottie smiled. "Mostly we gossiped and talked about what we would have been had we not settled in Whiskey Gulch."

"I believe Mom was happy here. And that had everything to do with her dear friends." Matt stood and pulled the two women into a big hug. "I love you two like you were family."

Dottie and Barb brushed tears from their eyes.

"Sweetie, you are family," Dottie said.

"Family." Barb sniffed. "I've got something in my eye. I'd better go check on it."

"Me too," Dottie said, and hurried back to the kitchen after Barb.

"It's almost seven o'clock," Aubrey reminded Matt.

He pulled out his wallet and slapped a few twenties on the table.

Aubrey would have added a couple of her own, if she could have spared them. The ladies were lovely, and they truly cared about their friend and her son.

And they didn't know their friend as well as they might have thought. Lynn Hennessey hadn't told them about the people she was helping escape a terrible life they would have been sentenced to had the coyotes sold them to the highest bidders.

Chapter Seven

Matt held the driver's side door for Aubrey as she climbed in behind the steering wheel. After he got in the passenger side, she shifted into Drive and pulled out of the parking lot, headed back to his auto shop and their meeting with Juan Salazar.

At the shop, Matt helped Aubrey out of the Jeep, noting again the dark circles beneath her eyes. "There's a couch in my office if you want to lie down while we wait for Juan."

She shook her head. "Thank you, but I think I'll stay on my feet. If I go down, I might not get up for the next forty-eight hours. We have a little girl to find. The sooner we get on it, the better."

"Fair enough." He wouldn't talk her into resting until the child was recovered. "I'm going to open this place up like I plan on working. I don't want Juan to think it's all about the questions I want to ask."

"Go," she said. "Do what you have to do. In the

meantime, I'll call the sheriff's office and see if they've learned anything about the people who killed Rosa and attacked my—your mother's cottage. Maybe the guy you shot has come to in the hospital and confessed."

"We can always dream," Matt said, his tone flat. The chances of the guy he shot confessing to shooting a woman were slim to none. Not when he was probably in the country illegally, and murder, no matter his nationality, was punishable by death in the state of Texas. Not to mention, the people he was working with would just as soon kill him to keep him from saying anything about their organization, or where they hid the girls they kidnapped.

Matt hit the button to open the overhead door to the repair bay where he had a car up on one of the two hydraulic lifts. He was working on rebuilding the transmission and replacing the oil pan in this one. Thankfully, the owner wasn't in a hurry to get it back. He would be out of town for the next two months, working on the oil pipeline as a safety inspector.

Since he'd inherited half the Whiskey Gulch Ranch, Matt had cut back on the work he did at his auto shop. He'd wanted to spend time learning the business of ranching, but that, too, was on hold until he solved the mystery of his mother's death. He'd just cracked the cold case files when he'd nearly run into Aubrey on the highway going home to the ranch.

By helping Aubrey, he had a feeling he might uncover the secrets of his mother's murder. The house of angels was his clue, and a pretty big one at that.

The overhead door had just ground to a halt above when Juan Salazar pulled up in a pickup that had seen much better days on the outside.

Matt knew the engine, though, and it was in prime condition, having been replaced by an engine Juan had found in a junkyard. All it needed was a few new gaskets, belts and a thorough flush of the oil and transmission fluid and it had hummed like a brand-new motor. Matt suspected Juan liked driving around in the junky-looking truck because he could negotiate better prices from the owners of the yards for the parts he pulled himself. And, for the most part, he did get better prices and passed them on to his customers, like Matt who rebuilt engines for people who couldn't afford to pay the big bucks it would take to send a vehicle to a dealership's auto repair service.

No, Matt had started his business to make money, but not at the expense of those who didn't have the money to spend. He looked for every way to cut expenses so that the old ladies, single mothers and guys out of work could get their cars fixed at the lowest possible cost. And if someone couldn't pay, he always gave them the option to pay him in trade. A batch of cookies here, sweep the garage for another account or a few parts pulled from the local junkyard.

He'd bartered with Juan on numerous occasions. He considered the man a friend. He hoped he didn't damage their friendship by asking questions Juan might consider too personal or dangerous. No matter what it did to their friendship, he'd still probe. A little girl's life hung in the balance. Anything Juan might know could help them in their search for Isabella.

Juan climbed out of his pickup and reached into the back for a dirty cardboard box and an even dirtier oil pan.

"Oh, good." Matt took the box with the oil pan from the man and studied it briefly. It appeared to be a perfect match for the one he was replacing. "Thanks. What do I owe you?"

Juan gave him the price. Matt reached into his wallet and paid him cash. He always paid in cash, knowing Juan preferred to work on that basis. He barely made enough money to feed his wife and six children, and giving half of his money to the government in taxes meant his children might go hungry.

Juan pocketed the money and then looked at

Matt. "Why did you ask me to come earlier? You don't appear to be working on this job today."

Matt should have known the parts dealer would see through his ruse and call him on it. He decided truth was his best option to get the answers he needed and to retain his friendship with this man who only wanted to provide for his family.

"You heard about my mother's house on Maple Street?" Matt asked.

Juan stiffened. "I had nothing to do with what happened."

Matt gave the other man a half smile. "I didn't expect you had. You're a good man, and a good friend. You also know a lot of people in this area. I thought you might know who did participate in the attempt to kill me and my date, Aubrey Blanchard."

Juan spun and walked toward the bay door.

"Juan," Matt called out. "I need your help. If you know anything about these people, I could really use a clue. They killed a woman and took her small daughter. They would have taken the woman's baby, too, if Ms. Blanchard hadn't gotten to it first, while taking a large stick to three of the men involved."

A smile tugged at Juan's mouth. "Your woman hit them?" His smile faded. "Good for her. And bad for her. They don't forgive and they never forget."

Now he was getting somewhere. Matt waved Juan deeper into the shop. "You should come inside. If anyone is watching, I don't want them to think you're discussing anything but the part you brought me and any other automobile parts I might want you to be on the lookout for."

Juan frowned. "I want to make it clear. I don't know anything." He started to walk back to the parking lot where he'd left his truck.

"The little girl's name is Isabella. Her baby sister is Marianna. They lost their mother. Please don't let them lose each other," Matt pleaded. "Anything you might know that could lead us to where they might be holding the girl might mean the difference between life and death for that child."

Juan stood with his back to Matt. He didn't move, but he didn't speak either.

"Juan, how old is your little girl?" Matt asked, knowing it was playing dirty to throw Juan's family into the conversation. "What if someone took her? Wouldn't you do anything, including moving heaven and earth, to find her?"

"She's four. And yes." Juan spun to face him. "My Lucinda is everything to me. If someone took her, I'd do anything to get her back. Then I'd injure the bastards who took her, and I'd leave their bodies where the buzzards could pick their flesh from their bones one bite at a time…while they were still alive." His face twisted into a mask of anger. "I'd want them to feel all the pain and know that what they'd done was wrong."

"You concur that men who steal children and sell them into the sex trade are the lowest of despicable life?" Matt asked.

"Yes," Juan agreed adamantly.

"Then please—" Matt reached out to touch the man's arm "—tell me anything you know. I promise not to reveal my source."

Juan looked to the corner of the ceiling, his jaw firm. "They will know."

"If we get info from another source, they'll still suspect you and anyone else they think caught a whiff of something. At least if you help us, we can put them away faster. After we free the girl. I want to corner them and watch their faces as we show them what happens to men who trade in human flesh." He drew in a breath and let it out. "Right now, what we're most concerned about is helping Isabella. We have to find her before they complete the deal. If it's not already too late."

Juan looked at the car on the lift for a long time without saying a word. Then he closed his eyes and pinched the bridge of his nose. "What other parts do you need from me?"

"Just one," Matt said. "The part that helps me find a little girl."

Juan dropped his hand to his side. "It could take a while for me to locate that part."

"I don't have a lot of time," Matt said. "The longer I wait, the less likely I will be able to fix the problem."

Juan nodded. "I'll do my best to locate the part in the least amount of time. Sometimes the parts aren't where they were before. But I have sources who can help me find them where they are."

Matt nodded, understanding Juan's need to speak in shoptalk. If anyone happened by and overheard them talking, they could be the next victims of the coyote killers.

Juan returned to his truck.

Matt followed and stood by the driver's window. "Thank you my friend. I look forward to hearing from you about that part." He held out his hand.

Juan reached through the window and shook Matt's hand. "I'll be in touch."

"Thank you." At least he'd gotten a commitment out of Juan. Unfortunately, his friend hadn't known where Isabella was being held.

Yet.

Knowing Juan, he'd get that information from his vast connections and pass it back to him.

Matt prayed it didn't get Juan into trouble with

the coyote men in the process. He hadn't wanted to put the family man in danger, but they had to take some risks in order to find the little girl as quickly as possible.

"What did your friend have to say?" Aubrey stepped out of Matt's office, slipping her cell phone into her back pocket. He knew she'd wanted to be part of the conversation, but it was probably better he talked to the man alone.

"He didn't know where they were keeping Isabella, but he has contacts and will tap on them and see what they know," Matt drew her into his arms. Holding her was as natural to him as breathing. "What did the sheriff have to say?"

Aubrey sighed and leaned her forehead against his chest. "They followed the ATV tracks in the field where Rosa was shot. They led to a dirt road where we assume the ATVs were loaded onto a trailer and taken away, either to be stashed in dense foliage, or transported back to whatever hiding place they've commandeered."

"Which leads us where?" he whispered, smoothing a hand over her auburn hair.

"Nowhere. Absolutely nowhere." Aubrey curled her fingers into Matt's shirt. "I can't imagine what Isabella is going through right now. She must be frightened out of her mind."

Matt's chest tightened at the sob in Aubrey's voice. "We have to have faith that we'll find her.

And we have to keep looking." He tipped her chin up and stared down into watery eyes. "We'll find her," he said. How, he wasn't sure, but he had to do his best. For Isabella. For Marianna. For Aubrey. For his mother—the angel in the casa, helping those who couldn't help themselves.

Chapter Eight

Aubrey drove out to the Whiskey Gulch Ranch, following Matt's directions, eager to see more clearly the spread the town was named after and the people she'd barely met but heard so much about already.

"Wasn't the senior Mr. Travis murdered recently?" she asked as they passed through the gate and started down the long, curving drive through a stand of gnarled scrub oak trees. They emerged from the trees to be flanked on both sides by wide-open pastures dotted with horses and cattle. Once again, they entered a stand of trees to emerge a minute later into the bright Texas sunshine. Ahead was a green, grassy knoll upon which stood a rambling house made of white limestone and cedar timbers. Wide porches wrapped around the house with swings and rocking chairs inviting tired hands to rest a spell. Aubrey hadn't been to the house in the daylight. It was welcoming at night, but even more so in the light of day.

The place beckoned Aubrey to come, sit on the porch and drink iced tea. She could feel the peace and tranquility of it and was glad she'd be staying there for a few days. At least until they found Isabella and brought the murderers to justice.

If they didn't do both, the coyotes would continue to prey on the innocent and more children would be lost.

As she pulled to a stop in front of the house, Mrs. Travis emerged onto the front porch and hurried down the steps toward them.

"Oh, my dear Ms. Blanchard," she said without preamble. "I'm so sorry you've had to go through such a terrible night." She engulfed Aubrey in a warm hug that made her feel like part of the family.

"Call me Aubrey," she said.

"Please, call me Rosalynn," Mrs. Travis said.

"How's the baby?" Aubrey asked, looking past Rosalynn to the house.

Lily came out on the porch carrying Marianna, balancing a baby bottle beneath her chin.

Rosalynn laughed. "Marianna is doing great. She misses her mother, but she's taking to the bottle of formula like a champ."

Aubrey climbed the steps to the porch.

"Do you want to hold her?" Lily asked.

The ache in her heart was so strong, it nearly brought her to her knees. "Yes, please."

Rosalynn waved a hand toward one of the rocking chairs. "Take a seat and Lily can hand you the baby and the bottle."

Aubrey dropped into a rocking chair, her knees feeling suddenly weak. She held out her arms as Lily laid the baby in them.

Marianna took a shaky breath and went back to sucking on the bottle, her eyes blinking sleepily.

Holding a baby and feeding her a bottle felt natural and strange at the same time. Aubrey had breastfed Katie until she was able to eat solid foods. As Marianna sucked on the bottle, Aubrey stared at the dark-haired baby, as different from Katie as night and day. Katie had a light dusting of peach fuzz when she was born but didn't get a full head of hair until nearly four years old.

Marianna had thick rich black hair and dark brown eyes. The babies were quite different, and both absolutely beautiful in their own way.

Aubrey swallowed the lump rising in her throat. Now wasn't the time to let her emotions get the better of her.

"Hey, sweet Marianna," she whispered. "I'm glad to see you're doing well. We're going to find your sister and bring her home to you. Did you know that?"

"The sheriff's department contacted the Customs and Border Patrol about Marianna. Health and Human Services department are on their way to collect her. She'll need to be evaluated for overall health and given appropriate vaccinations before her uncle can collect her."

"Poor baby," Aubrey cooed. "Gonna be poked and prodded and no mama to hold you and tell you everything will be all right." Those tears she'd been holding tight slipped free. "Now, look at me, getting you all wet." She laughed on a sob.

"Hopefully, we will have found her sister by the time Marianna goes home to her uncle in Hico," Matt said. "In the meantime, what room do you want me to put Aubrey's things in?"

Rosalynn smiled. "I've got one ready. Do you need help with her bags?"

"No," Matt said. "She only had two."

Rosalynn frowned. "Only two?" She turned her glance to Aubrey. "I thought you'd be staying with us for longer than that."

Aubrey chuckled. "I only have two bags' worth of things," she said. "You could say I'm going with the minimalist approach."

"Oh, sweetie," Rosalynn said. "I hope you make Whiskey Gulch your home and collect a lot more than just two bags. It's not a bad place to live. Like anywhere, a very few people make it miserable for the majority. I have faith this will resolve, and life will get back to normal."

Aubrey didn't mention that it seemed to be a recurring theme. As her hostess, Rosalynn didn't need another reminder of the loss of her husband.

"Do you want me to take Marianna while you get your things settled?" Lily asked.

"As much as I'd love to just hold her, I need to shower and change into my scrubs. I have a patient who will be waiting for me to help her with her lunch and meds at noon." Aubrey reluctantly handed Marianna to Lily.

"I'm glad you'll be staying for a while," Lily said. "It's nice to have another woman around the house to keep me and Rosalynn company."

Trace stepped out onto the porch and slipped an arm around his fiancée. "What? Are you telling me you don't enjoy talking about guns and deer hunting?"

"Of course, but I also enjoy talking about hair, nails, fashion and the best time of the month to try to get pregnant."

Trace sputtered. "What?" He shook his head. "Don't you think I would be interested in a subject like that?"

Lily's lips twitched. "Which subject? Hair and nails?"

He glared at her. "You know damn well the

pregnancy subject. Seeing as I'd have to go along with whatever plan you cook up." His brow eased and he smiled down at her. "You do look good with a baby in your arms."

"And so will you," she said. "Plan on a fifty-fifty split of diaper changes when we have one of our own."

Trace crossed his arms over his chest. "I can handle that."

His mother snorted. "We'll see. He couldn't clean up puppy poop without gagging as a child."

"Mom, I'm not a child anymore. I've dealt with much worse."

"Uh-huh," she said, a knowing smile curling her lips.

Holding a baby had reminded Aubrey how much she'd loved being a mother. Though the thought of bringing another baby into the world scared her to death. How could she willingly bring a child into a world where evil men existed to prey on small innocents? The odds of it happening again were slim, but wait… Here she was again, searching for a missing little girl.

Aubrey pushed to her feet, her body protesting at the lack of sleep. A shower should wake her enough to see this one patient. Then she'd get to work searching for more clues as to the whereabouts of Marianna's sister. She hoped Matt's contact would come through by then and they could raid whatever building they were keeping the little girl in.

Matt hurried out to her Jeep and returned with her two bags.

Aubrey followed Rosalynn up the stairs and to the right.

"We built onto the original house, hoping to fill it with little ones. Alas, James and I were only gifted with one child, Trace. Seemed such a waste to have so many bedrooms and so few people in them." She paused in front of one door and smiled. "Now I'm glad we added the rooms. With Trace home, Lily working for us, Irish working for the ranch and the protection service Trace is starting up, and Matt and now you, we have plenty of room for all of you."

She pushed open the door to a room with a queen-size bed draped in soft gray-blue and white tones. The filmy curtains over the widows muted the sun's rays, while allowing enough light to fill the space.

"This is lovely," Aubrey said. "Thank you for letting me stay while we're searching for Isabella."

"And you'll stay through the cottage renovations, won't you?" Rosalynn prodded.

"We'll see. I don't want to impose on your kindness," Aubrey said.

"No imposition at all," Rosalynn assured her.

"Everyone helps around here, so it's not a chore to keep up with the place."

"I fully expect to help. And pay rent. I can't expect to live here free of charge."

"Don't be ridiculous." Rosalynn waved a hand. "Trace and Matt can afford to pay the utilities."

"That's not the point. I like my independence. It's important to me."

"Then take the rent out in trade. Cook a meal every once in a while or clean a stall. I can tell you now, Matt won't take your money. He's probably feeling responsible for what happened to his mother's house and the fact you've been displaced because of it." She smiled at Matt, who'd just entered the room with Aubrey's bags. "Is that right?"

"Don't go putting words in my mouth," he grumbled. "But yes. Rosalynn is right. You can't live in my mother's house while it's being repaired. Since you're here, rather than move again, you might as well stay until the repairs are complete."

Aubrey looked from Matt to Rosalynn and back. "You're not going to let me change your mind?"

Matt and Rosalynn shook their heads simultaneously.

"Okay. But if you get tired of me, all you have

to do is tell me. I can find somewhere else to live for a few weeks."

"Now that we've settled your temporary living arrangements," Rosalynn said, "the bathroom is across the hall. There are towels in the cabinet behind the door. Help yourself. I'll have ham sandwiches waiting when you're done in the shower. All I need to know is do you prefer mayo or mustard?"

"Mustard," Aubrey said.

"I prefer mustard as well," Matt said as he set the two cases on the end of the bed.

"I wasn't asking you," Rosalynn said. "You can make your own sandwich."

"Yes, ma'am. I guess my guest status has reached a limit," he said with a wink.

She gave a firm nod. "You bet. You're one of us, now."

"I'll take it," he said, and hugged her.

Rosalynn's cheeks reddened. "I wish your father could have known you were his son while you were growing up. You're not as bad as you had the town believe."

"I'm glad the act I put on worked." He scooted out the door of Aubrey's bedroom and stood in the hallway. "My room is next to yours, if you need anything."

Aubrey nodded. "Thanks for bringing my things up."

"I'm going to make a sandwich. With mustard."

"Leave us some of that ham," Rosalynn called out after him.

Matt left the two women, his feet clattering down the steps to ground level.

"That boy," Rosalynn said with a twisted smile. "I believe I love him like my own."

Aubrey didn't remark on the fact the older woman had called Matt a boy. He was anything but. Pure, adult male was a better description of the muscular man who appeared tough with his leathers and motorcycle but underneath was gentle and caring. "Thank you for showing me the room and letting me stay."

"Oh, the ranch isn't mine. It's up to the new owners, Trace and Matt, who stays and who goes."

"I would have thought ownership would have passed to you, after your husband's death," Aubrey said.

Rosalynn smiled. "I didn't want the headache. I wouldn't let James leave it to me. I asked for a nest egg of money and to be free of managing the land and people."

"You're smart and strong enough to manage his ranch," Aubrey pointed out.

"I know that, but I don't have the drive and determination of Trace and Matt. If they keep it, they'll take it to the next level. They're sharp, driven, and the competitive spirit will keep them looking for more sustainable ways for this land to pay for itself and its upkeep. As long as they own it, I have a place to stay. I hope they choose to bring me grandchildren to spoil."

"That would be lovely," Aubrey said.

"Either way, I'm not sweating it," Rosalynn said. "If they sell, I'll buy a place in the Florida Keys and sit on the beach, drinking mai tais. I'll miss the home I shared with my late husband. Truthfully, the place isn't the same without him. A change of scenery might be the trick to help me through my grief."

Aubrey touched the woman's arm. "I'm so sorry for your loss."

Rosalynn patted her hand. "Don't you worry about me. You have enough on your plate. Speaking of plates, I need to go make some sandwiches." The matriarch left the room and headed down the stairs.

Aubrey unpacked enough clothes to locate her underwear and a set of scrubs. With her toiletries kit in her hand, she crossed the hallway to the bathroom on the other side, entered and locked the door behind her. Fifteen minutes later, she'd showered, washed the dirt and dust from her body and hair, dressed in her blue scrubs and pulled her wet hair into a bun at the nape of her neck. As an afterthought, she dabbed on a little mascara and a light shade of lipstick, hoping that if she looked good, she'd feel good.

Ah, who was she kidding? She wanted to look good for the next time she saw Matt. But not too made up, or she'd appear to be trying too hard.

Trying what?

She paused with her hand on the doorknob.

Did she want Matt to notice her? Hadn't he already done that? Hell, he'd kissed her. Yes, it was a light brush of the lips, probably in the heat of the moment after being shot at. Anyone would have done that as a celebration of having lived through a horrendous attack.

If she were honest with herself, she'd admit… She wanted him to kiss her again.

Aubrey closed her eyes. What was she thinking? The ink on her divorce papers was barely dry, even though she'd been in the process of getting that divorce for over a year. Her marriage had ended long ago. The day Katie disappeared out of her front yard and her husband blamed her.

The fact was, she had no business being interested in another man. She was content to live alone and piece her life back together. She had no business bringing her baggage into a relationship. It wouldn't be fair to the man, and she wasn't sure she could hold up her end of the emotions.

She turned back to the mirror, pulled a tissue

out of the box on the counter and rubbed the lipstick off her mouth. The mascara would take too long, so she left it. A quick glance at her watch told her she barely had time to grab a bite of the sandwich Rosalynn was preparing for her before she had to leave.

Mrs. Blair would be happy to see her and want to hear all the news from outside her house. The woman had been convalescing at a nursing home after hip surgery but had been discharged to continue her recovery at home. Unfortunately, she had no relatives to help her through the rest of her rehab or to encourage her to do her physical therapy exercises. It was Aubrey who came to help her do the things she wasn't quite up to yet, like a little house cleaning, filling her pill container and taking her vitals. The woman looked forward to the visits and thanked her for taking the time to help her.

Satchel in hand, Aubrey found her way to the kitchen, where a place had been set at the large kitchen table with a ham sandwich on a plate, several bags of potato chips for her to choose from and a large glass of iced tea.

"I didn't know if you like sugar in your tea, or if you like it unsweetened," Rosalynn said. "So, it's unsweetened."

"Perfect," Aubrey said with a smile and took her seat.

Matt sat across the table from her, already halfway through a sandwich of his own. He had a little spot of mustard on the corner of his mouth.

Aubrey didn't know whether to tell him about it or let it go. The problem was, she couldn't look away. She found herself wanting to lick that dab of mustard off his lip. The thought sent a rush of warm awareness throughout her body. What would he think of her if she got up, walked around the table, sat in his lap and cleaned that mustard off his mouth with her tongue? That warmth she'd been feeling flared into a wildfire. Hell, while she was at it, she could whisper in his ear... *Kiss me.*

"What?" he said, yanking her back to reality.

Heat shot up her neck and into her cheeks. "Did I say something?" God forbid she'd whispered "kiss me" out loud. Seriously, the man had her tied in knots. And he didn't even know it.

"No, but you're looking at me kind of funny," he said. "Do I have something on my face?"

Rosalynn leaned over the table at that moment to collect the unopened bags of chips. "You have mustard on the side of your mouth."

He brushed his thumb across the offending dab and popped the thumb into his mouth to lick it off. "Thanks."

Given the way he dealt with the mustard, he'd shifted Aubrey's thoughts from the corner of his mouth to the thumb that had gone in to be licked. Now all she could think of was what his tongue would feel like against her skin.

Focus, woman.

"Any word from the sheriff's office?" she asked and then took a bite of the sandwich, glad to look away from the handsome man sitting across from her.

"Nothing," Matt said, polishing off the rest of his ham sandwich. "And nothing from Juan. I hope to hear from him soon. If I know Juan, he's on it. He loves his family and his little girl. The thought of another little girl, much like his own, being held captive with the intent to sell her to some evil sex trader or pimp has to gnaw at his gut as much, if not more so, than it gnaws at ours. I expect to hear from him soon."

Aubrey chewed on the bite she'd taken, wishing she hadn't started it. Her belly was knotted. Eating wasn't helping. She glanced at the clock on the wall, glad for an excuse to leave. "Rosalynn, the sandwich is really good. Do you have something I can wrap it in? I really have to get going, or I'll be late."

Rosalynn took her plate. "Don't you worry about it. I can wrap it up for you, if you'd like to take it with you or keep it for later."

"Later, please. I don't know how long I'll be

gone, and I don't want it to go bad sitting in my Jeep getting hot."

"I'll wrap it and put it in the refrigerator where you can find it later." Rosalynn carried the plate to the counter and covered the sandwich in cellophane, then placed it in the refrigerator.

Aubrey gathered her satchel in her hand and pushed to her feet. "I'd better get going, or I'll be late."

Matt stood. "I'm ready whenever you are."

"I just want to brush my teeth and wash my hands," Aubrey said.

"Same." Matt followed her up the stairs.

They parted in front of their doors and went in for their respective toothbrushes.

Both appeared again at the same time.

"You keep your toothbrush in your bedroom instead of the bathroom?" she asked.

He shrugged. "It's a habit from my time in the Marines. You never left your toothbrush in the bathroom." He gave her a wry grin. "Someone might use it to scrub a toilet."

Aubrey grimaced. "I can see why it became a habit."

Matt waved a hand toward the bathroom. "You first."

"That's not necessary. There are two sinks. If washing your hands and brushing your teeth is all you want to do, we can do it together and save time." She entered the bathroom and chose the farthest sink from the door.

Within seconds they were brushing their teeth in rhythm with each other.

Aubrey found it strangely warm and reassuring, like an old married couple. When she was finished, she washed her hands and stowed her toothbrush in its case.

Matt stood at the door, his brow twisted. "Did that feel as strange to you as it did to me?"

"I'm sorry," she said. "Next time we can brush separately."

"No, not strange bad," he said. "More like strange in that I felt like we were an old married couple, comfortable in brushing our teeth together, that we'd known each other a long time."

She smiled. "That's exactly what I was thinking. And we barely know each other."

"I believe when people go through a traumatic experience together, it brings them closer faster. You skip all the getting-to-know-each-other-slow pace and go right to being close and in tune with the other, automatically."

"Really? Considering the only other traumatic experience I've endured is the loss of my daughter. It had the opposite effect on me and my husband."

"Ah, but then you weren't strangers. I've seen this effect in the battlefield. New members of a team bond overnight in a skirmish. Then they're friends for life."

"Is that the difference?" Aubrey asked. "They have to be strangers?"

He nodded. "Of course, I don't have a doctorate in psychology to back up my theory, but I've seen it on more than one occasion." He grinned and waved her through the door. "I figure fifteen minutes of being fired on was like condensing a full year of getting to know each other. At least that's my story and I'm sticking to it."

Aubrey laughed. "I like that story. That means we're no longer strangers."

"We've shared a moment," Matt said. "Not a particularly pleasant moment but one that has defined us as more than strangers. I'd like to think we could be friends now."

Aubrey nodded. "We could be that." She tapped her toothbrush case against the tube of toothpaste she'd brought with her. "I'll just put this in my room."

Matt nodded. "Me too."

They ducked in at the same time and emerged again, as if on cue.

Matt chuckled. "See? We're even in sync with each other."

Aubrey smiled. "Yes, we are." Her smile faded. "I'd better be going."

"I'm going with you."

"I'm not sure that's a good idea. Mrs. Blair isn't up to visitors, and she might get flustered having a stranger in her house."

"Mrs. Blair?" His brow dipped. "As in Mrs. Blair the high school history teacher?"

"I believe she was a teacher before she retired."

"I had her in high school. She was tough, but good. I actually came out of her class with a good understanding of why we study history and why it's important."

Aubrey checked her watch. "I need to get moving. I'm sure Mrs. Blair wouldn't remember you from high school. She had a lot of students since you were there. And I'd bet you don't look like you did back then."

"I think she will remember me. I was teacher's pet for the only time in my life." He grinned. "I'm going, Aubrey," he said, his expression serious. "Even if I wait in the Jeep for you to finish up."

Aubrey sighed. "I haven't let anyone push me around since I divorced my husband. And I promised myself I would never let that happen again." She paused. "That being said, I know you're only trying to protect me. So, I'll let it slide this time."

She led the way out of the house and climbed into the Jeep.

Matt got in on the passenger side and buckled his seat belt.

Aubrey liked making her own decisions, but she was glad Matt was with her. After the shootout that morning, she wasn't sure she could go anywhere on her own without feeling exposed and vulnerable.

She prayed they found Isabella soon. Aubrey hoped that when they did rescue the little girl, they'd find a way to stop the people who were responsible for Rosa's death and the kidnapping.

Chapter Nine

The drive to Mrs. Blair's house a couple miles out of town from the ranch took thirty minutes. It was noon when Aubrey pulled up in front of her patient's home and killed the engine.

"Let me check with her to see if she's up for visitors." Aubrey got out of the Jeep and carried her satchel up to the house. After a brief knock she heard Mrs. Blair call out, "Come in, Aubrey."

Mrs. Blair was up with her walker, moving slowly toward the kitchen.

Aubrey smiled. "Look at you, getting around on your own."

"I decided it was time I got back in shape. I'm thinking of competing in one of those Iron Woman competitions. She pulled two cups from a cabinet and set them on the counter. "Do they have categories that go up to my age?"

"Actually, they do. You're not that old. You just have some challenges to overcome."

"I've decided you're right. And I'm ready

to overcome them and rejoin the human race. Only in my case, the human walkathon. The Iron Woman race might be a little out of my league."

"Baby steps, Mrs. Blair. You'll get there with baby steps."

The older woman shook her head. "I shouldn't be this crippled at my age. I'm not even eighty yet. I've got a lot of years left in me. Did you know my mother lived to be ninety-nine and three-quarters?"

"I did not know that," Aubrey said, pulling her blood pressure cuff out of her satchel.

"She died a couple months short of her one hundredth birthday. She fell and broke her hip, was laid up and got pneumonia. And I had high hopes of drinking a beer with her at her birthday party."

"All the more reason to get back to normal. You can't have a beer while on some of this medication. Especially the pain relievers," Aubrey said.

"That's good, because I haven't been taking them. Figured it was time to pull up my big girl panties and make this new hip work for me."

Aubrey glanced out the window at her Jeep. "Mrs. Blair, how are you for company today?"

"I'm great. I've got you."

"I mean for more than me," Aubrey said.

Mrs. Blair's white brows rose. "You got someone in mind?"

"As a matter of fact, I have someone waiting in my Jeep. He said he was a student of yours and that you'd remember him."

Mrs. Blair grimaced. "I had so many students—they blur in my mind."

"That's what I told him." Aubrey laughed. "He said you'd remember him. He was teacher's pet."

"The only teacher's pet I remember was that Hennessey kid. He liked to think he was a badass, but I saw right through him. He was one of the kindest young men I ever had the pleasure of teaching history."

"Guess I'll be eating my words today," Aubrey said with a grin. "The person out in my Jeep is Matthew Hennessey, your number one teacher's pet."

"You're not pulling this old woman's leg, are you?" She aimed her walker toward the front of the house, her gaze on the Jeep. "Why would a handsome young man like that come visit an old lady like me?"

"He's accompanying me today."

Her gaze turned from the Jeep to Aubrey. "Well, now, that makes more sense. But don't deprive me of some eye candy. He might have been a student a long time ago, but he's mighty fine-looking. I'm old, not dead, as far as I can tell."

"Promise me you won't turn backflips when I bring him in?" Aubrey teased.

"I promise," the older woman said. "I might pinch him, though. Just to make sure he's real and not a figment of my imagination."

Aubrey went to the door and waved for Matt to come in.

Mrs. Blair hurried back to the kitchen, as fast as she could maneuver the walker. "I'll need another cup for tea."

"You could let me do that for you, you know," Aubrey said.

"I could, but that would defeat my goal of being able to take care of myself." She fished a cup out of the cabinet. "I'm tired of my own company and ready to start driving and volunteering for something."

"Thinking of volunteering at the school? I bet they'd be happy to have you back."

"No, I was thinking of something more exciting." Mrs. Blair set the kettle on her stove and switched on the gas. "Think they need help at the local food bank, or better yet, the sheriff's office?"

"I don't know. But it wouldn't hurt to ask. It would give you a good reason to go to town and get some social interaction." Aubrey opened the door for Matt. "I stand corrected."

Matt came in, filling the small house with his

broad shoulders and sexy smile. "You remembered me, didn't you, Mrs. Blair."

"Yes, I did. I couldn't forget my favorite student of all thirty-three years of my teaching career."

He went to her and engulfed her in a hug. "It's good to see you."

"And you," she said. "Are you trying to steal my pretty nurse away from me?"

"No, ma'am," he said, making sure she was steady on her feet before he let go. "I just came along for the ride. But when I heard she was coming to see you, I had to come say hello."

"I'm glad you did. I'm so tired of these walls. You're a breath of fresh air in this stuffy old house." She waved him toward the old-fashioned dinette table with the shiny red cushions. "Sit. I'm heating water. Would you like tea or a coffee? I have to warn you, I only have instant coffee. But I could sweeten it with a jigger of Baileys, if you like."

"Contributing to my delinquency, Mrs. Blair?" Matt asked.

"I can, now that you're not my student."

"Tea is fine with me," he said. "But why don't you let me get it while Ms. Blanchard gets your blood pressure."

"Oh, well, I guess she does need to do that before I start drinking tea with caffeine. Never could see the purpose of decaf tea," Mrs. Blair muttered as she shuffled toward the table and pulled out a chair. She sank onto the cushion and held out her arm to Aubrey.

"Me either. If I can't get my coffee in the morning, I go for the tea," Matt said.

Aubrey enjoyed the banter between Matt and Mrs. Blair. They were easy and comfortable with each other. She envied that closeness and hoped that someday, she'd be accepted as one of the locals.

While Aubrey took Mrs. Blair's vitals and recorded them in her chart, she asked her how she'd been feeling and her pain levels. When they were done, she packed up her tools.

"Matthew was my prize pupil. Not only was he attentive and curious, he helped one of my other students pass my class."

"How did he do that?" Aubrey asked.

"He tutored him after school."

Matt's lips twitched. "I threatened to hurt him if he told anyone that I was really a nice guy. I had a reputation to uphold as the meanest bad boy in town."

The kettle built up steam and let out a shrill whistle.

Mrs. Blair started to get up.

"Sit. I've got this," Matt said.

"When did you learn to be handy in the kitchen?" his old history teacher asked.

"In the Marine Corps," Matt said. "I had to figure out how to turn on the stove or starve. Chow hall food gets old real quick."

"So what are your plans for the rest of the day?" Mrs. Blair asked.

"We have to find a missing child," Matt answered.

Aubrey stood behind Mrs. Blair, shaking her head.

"Missing child?" the older woman looked from Aubrey to Matt and back. "What missing child?"

"Now, Mrs. Blair, you don't have to worry about this. We're working on it, as is the sheriff's department." Aubrey glared at Matt. "Why did you say anything?"

"Why shouldn't he?" Mrs. Blair demanded. "I would think everyone in the county should be out looking for the missing child." The older woman snagged Aubrey's arm. "Sit. Spill. Maybe I can help."

"How can you help?" Aubrey asked. "You can barely walk."

"I have a brain, don't I?" Mrs. Blair tapped her knuckles to the side of her head. "Last I knew, there wasn't a thing wrong with my mind. Tell me what's going on. If you don't, I'll hobble out to my car and drive myself into town and ask the sheriff."

"You can't drive yet. The doctor hasn't given you clearance to do so."

"My driver's license is still good. Nothing in the driver's manual says the doctor trumps the driver's license." She raised a challenging white brow. "Are you going to tell me, or am I going for a drive?"

Aubrey sighed and took the seat next to Mrs. Blair. Minutes later, she'd given the woman the digest version of what had happened over the past twenty-four hours.

Her first comment was, "You mean you and my Matt just met?"

"That's what you got out of all that?"

"You can't fault an old woman for thinking of the romantic element to this plot." Mrs. Blair shook her head. "From what I get out of all that is that you think the people who killed the mother and took Isabella might be hiding out somewhere in the vicinity of Whiskey Gulch."

Aubrey nodded. "The sheriff set up roadblocks and checkpoints on all roads leading out of Whiskey Gulch. They didn't have anyone come through who appeared to have kidnapped a child."

"That doesn't mean they didn't get through,

having hidden the girl in their trunk or a box or something," Mrs. Blair said.

"True," Aubrey said. "But we think they might be lying low until the heat cools and they can arrange to transport or conduct their trade."

"So, what have you done to locate their hideout?" Mrs. Blair asked, all business now.

"The sheriff is checking into all empty warehouses, houses, storage units in the area," Aubrey said. "He had volunteers out combing through the field and woods where the girl disappeared for clues about who might have taken her and where they might be keeping her hidden."

"I have a friend with connections in the Hispanic community with his ear to the ground, asking his sources for possible leads," Matt said.

"The longer she's missing, the more likely she won't be found."

Aubrey's breath lodged in her throat, threatening to choke her.

"What?" Mrs. Blair reached out to cover Aubrey's hand with hers. "You have to be realistic."

"We're going to find Isabella," Aubrey said. "We have to."

"This is personal, isn't it?" Mrs. Blair patted Aubrey's hand. "Okay, then, what are we going to do to find her?"

"Do you know any place in the county or surrounding counties where someone might hide a child?" Matt asked. "It might have to be big enough to hide their truck, trailer and four-wheelers, as well."

"Have they checked that old horse barn off the farm-to-market road west of town? They used to raise racehorses until they lost all their money and the bank foreclosed on them."

Matt pulled out his cell phone. "I'll ask the sheriff if they've checked it out." He texted the information to the sheriff. "Anything else you can think of?

Mrs. Blair drummed her fingers on the table, her gaze on the wall in front of her, her brow dented in concentration. "What about that old machine shop that used to make air compressor parts? They closed down several years ago, but as far as I know, the building is still there and unoccupied."

"We really should be going, anyway," Aubrey said. "You need rest. You've had an exciting hour and you're still recovering."

"Oh, pooh on that. This is the most excitement I've had in years. I'm sorry the little girl was lost, but I'd love to help find her. If I think of any other places, I'll let you know." She held out her hand. "Give me your cell phone number. I've lived in the area all my life. I think I've been on every road there is when my husband took me hunting. In my much younger days. As

I think of all the possible places, I'll send you a list of those sites. When you find the girl, let me know. I'll have her in my thoughts."

"Thank you, Mrs. Blair," Aubrey said. "Don't let this worry you too much. Believe me when I say, we're looking, and we won't give up until we find Isabella and reunite her with her baby sister."

Mrs. Blair rose from her chair.

Aubrey pushed the older woman's walker into her hands before turning toward the front of the house. "Don't overdo it, Mrs. B. I have another caregiver coming out for the rest of the week. I'm taking time off to help find the little girl. They'll take good care of you while I'm gone."

"Can't you just take care of me and leave the others to your counterparts?" Mrs. Blair asked. "I'll miss our chats. You're the only human contact I get."

"I promise to come back as soon as we find Isabella. I just can't do my job when I'm worried about that little girl." Aubrey touched Mrs. Blair's hand. "Besides, you're getting around better each day. You'll be driving yourself into town to volunteer and rejoin the community. Don't you have some friends from when you taught school?"

The older woman nodded. "Yes. But they're old. I need someone with more stimulating conversation. People who like to have fun and an occasional adventure."

Aubrey smiled. "You'll find that. Work that hip. I'll be back to help after we find Isabella."

"Are you sure you're not setting yourself up for disappointment?" Mrs. Blair asked. "Coyotes are good at hiding, sometimes in plain sight."

Her jaw firming, Aubrey shook her head. "We'll find her."

"Does this have to do with the child you lost?" Mrs. Blair asked, her voice softer.

Aubrey gasped. "How did you know about Katie?"

"I know how to search the internet for all kinds of information." She squeezed Aubrey's hand. "I also know what it's like to lose a child."

"You do?" Aubrey asked. She'd been seeing this woman for weeks and didn't know this about her.

Mrs. Blair nodded. "I lost my son in a drowning accident on a fishing trip. He was seventeen. He dived down to free the anchor from the brush it got tangled up in. My husband and I waited for him to come up. He never did."

"Oh, Mrs. Blair." Aubrey hugged the woman, tears in her eyes. "I'm so sorry."

"My husband and I blamed ourselves and second-guessed everything we could have done. But nothing we said or did could bring back our son."

She drew in a deep breath and let it out. "That was a long time ago, but it feels like yesterday." Mrs. Blair forced a smile to her face. "Look at me, making you sad when you needed cheering up." She leaned on her walker. "You two need to get out of here and find that child. She needs you more than I do. I'm on the mend and just around the corner from the freedom to drive again." She waved toward the door. "Go. And if I think of another place to look, I'll text you."

"Thank you, Mrs. Blair," Matt said. "It's been great seeing you. I'll be back to visit."

"Now that you know where I live and that I'm still alive?" She laughed. "You don't have to waste your time with an old lady like me. Not when you have a lovely young woman here to keep you company." She winked at Aubrey.

Aubrey's cheeks heated. "We're not dating."

"No?" Mrs. Blair's eyebrows rose. "Well, you should. You seem right for each other."

Matt chuckled. "Gave up teaching history for a new career in matchmaking, did you?"

The older woman shrugged. "Gotta have something to do. I don't have a classroom full of hellions to keep me entertained."

Matt hugged her. "Nevertheless, I'm sure we could have some pretty heated political debates. I'll be back."

She hugged him with one arm, holding on to

her walker with the other. "You're a good man, little Matthew Hennessey. I knew you were my favorite student for a reason. You have a big heart. Your classmates didn't see that. I did."

Mrs. Blair walked with them to the door, then looked up suddenly, as if remembering something. "You might also check with Rodney Morrison."

"The Realtor?" Matt asked.

She nodded. "If he's doing his job, he knows all the vacant residential and commercial properties in the area. They'd be potential listings. He's kinda full of himself, but talk to him."

Chapter Ten

Even after all those years, Mrs. Blair was just as sassy as ever. That was why he'd gotten along with her so well. She hadn't treated him as a child. More as an equal. She'd made his high school years much more tolerable.

Matt led the way out to Aubrey's Jeep and held the door while she climbed in.

Aubrey waited until he got in before she said, "So, you weren't such a bad boy as you thought you were back in high school, were you?" She shot him a look, cocking an eyebrow.

"I was bad enough to keep people at a distance, if I wanted to." He grinned. "And don't let ol' Mrs. Blair fool you. She was no saint. Her opinions were radical. She just didn't share them with many."

"And she shared them with you?"

He nodded. "Often. We had many a debate, after school."

"Are we going to check out the places she suggested?" Aubrey asked, shifting the Jeep into gear.

"We can bring it up to the sheriff. I don't feel comfortable poking around abandoned buildings with you when the guys who shot up your place might be there with fully loaded semiautomatic weapons."

"You have a good point." Aubrey shivered. "I don't know how you military guys can go into battle with bullets flying all around you."

"We did what we had to," Matt said, staring out the front windshield, images of past battles flooding his memories. "We didn't have anyone else to go in for us."

"I don't know why we didn't think of Mr. Morrison when he ran into us at the diner."

Matt's lip curled. "It was all I could do to tolerate him for more than the minute he interrupted our breakfast."

"He is a bit pushy," Aubrey said. "Do you think he'd heard about the trouble at your mother's house?"

"It's hard to say. He didn't mention it, but why single you out today, of all days?"

"Seems strange." Aubrey pulled out onto the highway and drove toward town. "That's the first time he's approached me since I came to Whiskey Gulch."

"His timing could be lousy, or he knew about

the attack this morning, but didn't say anything." Matt pulled out his cell phone and keyed a text message to Sheriff Richards.

"Who are you texting?" Aubrey asked.

"The sheriff. I'm passing on the sites Mrs. Blair suggested."

"Good. I'd rather he went out there with his deputies than us."

After he'd sent the message, his cell phone vibrated in his hand. Surely, the sheriff hadn't responded so quickly. He checked the incoming messages.

He had a cryptic note from Juan Salazar.

Old barn Glen and Hatcher Road junction fifteen minutes

"What is it?" Aubrey asked.

"Message from Juan. He wants us to go to the old barn at the junction of Glen and Hatcher Road."

Aubrey shook her head. "I don't know where that is."

"The turnoff for Hatcher is about a mile before you get to town."

"Tell me when we get close." She leaned toward the steering wheel, staring closely at the road in front of her, a frown denting her brow.

"Anyone tell you that you're cute when you frown?"

She shot a glance his way, her cheeks blossoming with color. "No."

"Well, you are." He faced the road. "Turn at the next road to your left. That's Hatcher."

Aubrey slowed the Jeep and took the turn onto Hatcher Road.

"The junction is about a mile from the main highway. I used to ride my motorcycle all over the county. It kept me from going stir-crazy."

"And yet, you returned to Whiskey Gulch?" Aubrey's brow twisted. "Why?"

Matt had asked himself the same question more than once. "I guess, it was the only home I ever knew. Once I got past the awkward teenage years, I realized part of the problems I had was me. I ran around with a chip on my shoulder, daring anyone to knock it off."

"Because you didn't have a father?"

He nodded. "They called me a bastard child. It made me mad. My mother didn't deserve the disdain others in the community showed her. She was a good person. No matter how ugly others were to her, she always showed kindness."

"She was the better person." Aubrey nodded toward the road ahead. "Is that the old barn?"

Matt nodded. "I don't see his truck. He might

have parked around the back of the building. Circle to the rear."

Aubrey pulled off the road onto a rutted path, leading to the barn. "I hope he doesn't expect us to go inside. That barn looks like a big wind will knock it over."

Matt nodded. The structure leaned. Many of the wood slats had long since rotted or were missing. The corrugated metal roof was missing several panels.

Aubrey drove the Jeep around the side of the building, bumping over the rough ground until she turned the corner.

Juan's beat-up old pickup was parked beside the building.

"You might want to stay in the Jeep. If anything happens, get out of here and go straight for the sheriff's office in town."

Aubrey frowned. "You think this is a setup?"

"No," he said. "I trust Juan. But after last night, I don't trust what I can't see. We could be watched, or someone could have followed us, though I didn't see anyone behind us as we turned off the highway."

"I'd rather go in with you."

Juan appeared at the door to the barn and beckoned them with a wave of his hand. Then he disappeared back into the shadowy structure.

"I'm going in," Matt said. He stuck his handgun in the pocket of his leather jacket and got out of the Jeep.

Aubrey met him at the front of the vehicle. "I'm going with you."

He hesitated. "I don't know if he'll be open with me if you come along."

"If it's a problem, I'll leave, and he can have you all to himself." She started for the barn. "Come on."

"For the record, I don't like this. You're putting yourself at risk."

"And so are you." She took his hand. "Let's do this together."

Against his better judgment, he walked with her into the darkness of the barn.

"Back here," Juan called out.

Matt pushed Aubrey behind him and advanced toward Juan's voice, moving slowly until his sight adjusted to the dim interior of the barn.

Rays of light knifed through missing boards, making the darkness even gloomier by contrast.

Matt shaded his eyes as he passed through the sun's rays and back into the shadows.

"Are you sure this barn isn't going to fall down on us?" Matt asked.

"You know as well as I do that this barn has been leaning for years. It will stand until we complete our business here."

Matt stopped in front of Juan and held out his hand.

Juan shook it, his brow furrowed in a worried frown. "My people in the barrio are scared," he said. "When I asked around about missing children, they stopped talking, went into their homes and closed the door in my face."

"I hope I haven't put you in danger."

"I'm afraid. For my family. Whoever is behind the kidnapping has powerful connections."

"What kind of connections?" Matt asked.

"Cartel connections," Juan said. "Los Zetas, based in Nuevo Laredo, has fingers reaching all the way up here in Whiskey Gulch. They're heavy into drug trafficking, human trafficking and gunrunning."

Matt's jaw tightened. "Thus the heavily armed men who tried to kill us with machine guns last night."

"They have a faction here. This area is a waypoint in their human trafficking operation. It's far enough from the border that the Customs and Border Patrol are fewer in this area and they've established drop spots to transfer their 'cargo' for further transport to buyers. There are people around here who help them in their efforts. Some who are paid to help, others who are blackmailed into helping. It's help or their families suffer. Most were afraid to speak to me for fear their children would be stolen and forced into the sex trade."

"Do you have any idea who is helping them, willingly?"

Juan shook his head. "None of my contacts would share that information. I don't know if that's because they really didn't know, or they were that afraid of repercussions. One person said it had to be someone most people trusted to be able to hide in plain sight."

"Did they give you any idea of where the waypoint is?" Aubrey asked.

Juan's lips thinned. "They said they move from place to place to keep anyone from noticing their activities. One of the places they used to use was this old barn. It was far enough off the road they wouldn't risk someone noticing a light burning inside."

Matt looked around the space with renewed interest.

"I've already looked all over this barn. There are no signs that it has been occupied recently. But this is the kind of place they are most likely to take advantage of."

"Off the beaten path and abandoned," Matt said. "Juan, are you going to be okay? Asking questions could stir the hornet's nest for you and your family."

Juan nodded. "I packed my wife and children

into the van today and sent them to Arkansas to visit my wife's sister for a week."

"What about you?"

"I want to find the missing little girl as much as you two," Juan said. "I couldn't look my wife and daughter in the eye without at least trying."

"Don't do anything that will put you at risk," Matt said. "Your wife and children need you alive."

He nodded. "I'm not staying at my house and I'm careful to vary my routes. I didn't spend six years running convoys through Iraq without learning a few things about avoiding enemy attacks."

Matt blinked. "I didn't know you'd been in the military." He realized he didn't know much about Juan and needed to remedy that as soon as possible.

"If you need a safe place to stay, go to the Whiskey Gulch Ranch. We have a security system and we will protect you there."

"I have a business to run. And I will not be frightened into hiding."

"Please consider hiding until we find these people and neutralize them," Matt urged his friend.

Juan shook his head. "I don't see you hiding."

"We have to find that little girl," Aubrey said.

Raising his hand like he was swearing an oath, Juan said, "And I vow to help in your search."

"For now, we'll have the sheriff check some of the abandoned buildings we think might be somewhere they would hide," Matt said. "Please, don't go looking on your own. If you actually stumble on their hideout, you'd be outnumbered and outgunned."

Juan nodded. "If I go looking, I'll do it from a distance, with a pair of binoculars."

"Be careful of perimeter guards and stay way back," Matt said.

"I will."

Matt held out his hand.

Juan put his in it and Matt pulled him into a hug. "Be careful, my friend."

"Y tu amigo." Juan turned to Aubrey. "Take care of this man. He's one of the good guys."

She smiled. "I'm beginning to figure that out. And I'll do my best."

Juan left the barn first and drove his truck back down Hatcher Road to the highway. Instead of turning right to go into Whiskey Gulch, he turned left and headed south.

Matt and Aubrey got into her Jeep and headed into Whiskey Gulch just as if they were returning from Mrs. Blair's house.

"I need to get some gas," Aubrey said.

"I'm buying," Matt insisted.

"I can pay for my own fuel," Aubrey said.

"I know you can, but you've been playing chauffeur to me. Let me do this."

Aubrey frowned. "When I left my marriage, I swore I'd never let myself become dependent on any man, ever again."

"I admire your spunk and determination. But, one tank of gas isn't becoming dependent." He grinned. "If it makes you feel better, I'll let you buy dinner. Don't get me wrong, though. It won't be a date. When I take a lady out on a date, I pay for dinner."

She lifted her chin, her mouth firm. "When we go out on a date, we'll go Dutch."

"I like that," he said with a smile. "*When* we go out on a date. Not *if*."

Her cheeks turned a pretty shade of pink. "I didn't mean to assume."

"Oh, assume all the way. I only wish I'd asked first." His grin broadened. "Because I will ask. And it's reassuring to know you'll say yes." He winked, liking the woman driving a lot more than he thought he'd ever like someone. She was strong, determined and had a heart big enough to risk her own life in an attempt to save the life of a stranger's child.

Aubrey pulled into the gas station and started to switch off the engine.

Matt caught her hand. "Leave it running."

"But the instructions say to turn it off."

"Given what we went through at your place early this morning, I'd like to keep it running in case we need to make a quick getaway."

Aubrey glanced around. "You think they'd be so bold as to attack us in broad daylight?"

"When we drove by the sheriff's office, I didn't see one service vehicle. I have a feeling they're all out checking abandoned structures in the county. I might be overreacting, but I'd feel better if you stayed in the vehicle and kept it running."

"When you put it that way…okay." She moved her hand back to the steering wheel and watched the road.

Matt slid his credit card into the machine and placed the nozzle in the tank. Soon, the pump had fuel flowing. All the while he kept watch on the main drag running through town.

As he finished up and was placing the nozzle back on the pump, his attention was on the machine. The squeal of tires down the block made his head jerk up.

A small dark car barreled down Main Street, aiming for the gas station where they were parked.

The driver wasn't slowing at all; in fact, he sped up the closer he got.

His heartbeat leaping into his throat, Matt yelled, "Aubrey, shift into Drive. Now!"

He could hear the gears shift.

"Go! Go! Go!" he yelled. He didn't have time to jump in.

A door flew open on the driver's side of the oncoming vehicle and a man dressed in black and wearing a black bandanna over his face threw himself out of the oncoming car.

As Aubrey gunned the accelerator, Matt dived away from the pumps.

AUBREY'S HANDS SHOOK as she slammed her foot down on the accelerator and the Jeep shot out of the gas station and onto the street. In her rear-view mirror, she saw Matt dive away from the pumps, as a vehicle slammed into them. An explosion rocked the earth and a huge fireball rose, engulfing the pumps where Matt had been standing moments before.

"Matt!" she screamed, and her foot left the accelerator.

The crack of gunfire sounded behind her.

A man dressed in black, wearing a black bandanna over his face, ran toward her, firing a handgun at her Jeep.

The back window exploded, sending shards of glass spraying over Aubrey's back. She mashed the gas pedal, sending the Jeep leaping forward.

More gunfire sounded behind her.

Matt emerged from the inferno of the gas pumps, firing his handgun at the man shooting at the Jeep.

Aubrey cried out, so relieved tears welled in her eyes.

The gunman jerked, fell to his knees and then toppled face-first onto the pavement. He lay still in the middle of Main Street.

Sirens sounded from the direction of the fire station. Within a few short minutes, an emergency vehicle raced toward the fire, followed by a large red fire truck.

Aubrey pulled to the side of the road and shifted into Park. She was shaking so hard, she waited a few seconds before getting out of the vehicle.

Matt pocketed his weapon, hurried toward the man lying in the middle of the street and waved the first responders over.

The firefighters dropped down from their truck and went to work containing the fire that had spread to the building beside the gas station.

EMTs rushed toward the gunman and started working to revive the man who'd tried to kill Matt and Aubrey.

Aubrey walked toward Matt. The closer she got, the faster she moved until she was running.

He met her halfway, his arms open.

She ran into them and was engulfed in his embrace.

"I thought you went up in the explosion," she said. Her voice cracked. She clung to him, her fingers curling into his shirt.

"I saw him coming and moved." He brushed her hair back from her face and stared down at her. "Thank you for doing exactly what I said." He shook his head. "If you hadn't, that car would have hit you first and slammed you into the pump." Matt kissed her forehead. "I don't even want to think about how that would have ended." He kissed her cheek. Then he kissed her lips, wrapping his arms around her, holding her so close.

Aubrey melted into him, a heat swelling inside her that had nothing to do with the nearby flames.

When the ambulance arrived, the EMTs loaded the man onto a gurney and into the back of the vehicle. About that time, Sheriff Richards arrived on scene.

Matt and Aubrey filled him in on what had happened before he spent a few minutes with the fire chief. When he was done, he returned to Matt and Aubrey.

"You two are a magnet for trouble," the sheriff said. "We were checking out the abandoned buildings you suggested when we got the call from dispatch that the gas station blew up." He shook his head. "I've been sheriff here for ten years and we've never had a gas station blow up. Nor have we had a house shot up like a scene from a Hollywood thriller."

"Trust me," Matt said. "We're not asking for it."

"I believe you," Sheriff Richards said. "I just wonder when your luck will run out."

Aubrey swallowed hard. Moments before, she'd thought Matt's luck had run out. Her heart had hurt so much, she'd had a hard time breathing.

"I hear you and your deputies have been out searching empty buildings," Matt said. "What did you find at those locations?"

The sheriff stared at the fire as the firefighters doused the flames on the convenience store gas station and the building beside it, bringing the fire under control. "We didn't find anyone in either location you proposed and a few others, including the warehouses by the railroad track."

Aubrey's hopes plummeted.

The sheriff turned back to them. "However, I found evidence that they had been there fairly recently in the old racehorse barn." He pulled a plastic bag containing a pink hair bow out of his pocket and held it up for them to see. "I found this and some food wrappers inside the building. I also found a spot where whatever truck they're using to haul those ATVs leaked oil on the floor of the barn. It was fresh. They moved not long ago."

Aubrey took the bag containing the bow from the sheriff's fingers and held it close to her pounding heart. "They were there. Isabella was there."

"We don't know that it was Isabella," the sheriff warned. "And we don't know where they moved her."

"Hopefully, not far," Aubrey whispered.

"We still have surveillance on all roads leading out of the area. If they try to leave, we should see them."

"Think they're waiting until the heat dies down to move?" Aubrey asked.

Sheriff Richards nodded. "That would be my bet. Or at least my hope."

"Have they gotten anything out of the man I tagged who shot up my mother's house?" Matt asked.

"He hasn't regained consciousness." The sheriff tipped his head toward the departing ambulance. "And your recent attacker isn't going to make it. They've got him on life support, but they think the doctor at the hospital will call it when he arrives."

Matt swore. "So, we're no closer to finding

Isabella or the people who are making our lives hell."

"Not at the moment," the sheriff said. "The fact we found evidence they were at the race-horse barn is encouraging. They're still out there and probably getting a little nervous. We just have to tighten the noose and flush them out." He frowned at Matt. "Please, don't go out look-ing at abandoned buildings. At the rate you're going, you're likely to run into the hornet's nest and get yourselves killed."

"We'll play it as safe as we can. So far the attackers have come to us, not the other way around." Matt's arm slipped around Aubrey's waist.

"Just so you know, I've asked the FBI and the DEA to get involved. They should arrive within the next hour."

"Good," Matt said. "I have it on good authority the people we're dealing with could be connected with *Los Zetas* out of Nuevo Laredo. Now would be a good time for the FBI, DEA and whatever other federal organization to step in and help us. This could be much bigger than your department can handle."

The sheriff nodded. "Exactly. I'd like to call in the National Guard and the Texas Rangers, as well. I saw what those thugs did to your mother's house. They're armed to the teeth. I don't want to sacrifice my people in a war where they're outnumbered and outgunned."

"With all those agencies converging on Whiskey Gulch, the cartel will be feeling the pinch. They might try to make a run for it before they get here."

"I thought of that. That's why I have all hands on deck on surveillance of the roads in and out of the area. I also have my techno-wizard of a nephew putting his drone in the air to make sure those guys don't try to make their escape cross-country. I've asked for the Customs and Border Patrol to back up my nephew with drones of their own. They should be here sometime this afternoon."

"Remember, if you need help, you have the men of Whiskey Gulch Ranch available to backfill. We're all trained in military special operations."

"I'll keep that in mind. We might have need of your services." The sheriff held out his hand. "For now, keep your heads down."

"Thanks, Sheriff. Same to you." Matt shook the man's hand and gathered Aubrey close.

"Ready to go to the ranch?"

She frowned. "I feel like we're close, like on the verge of finding Isabella. I hate to give up now."

"You heard the sheriff. He's calling in the big guns. The feds. When they get here, they'll take over and hopefully nail the bastards."

"And find Isabella. Alive." Aubrey leaned into Matt. "Is there anything else we can do right now? An abandoned building we can stake out? A contact we can lean on for information? Anything?"

Matt chuckled. "You don't give up, do you?"

She stopped and looked up into his eyes. "Not when a little girl's life is at risk."

"I'm not giving up either." He brushed his thumb over her cheek. "But after what happened this morning and now at the gas station, I'm afraid to take you with me. I'd feel much better if you stayed at the ranch."

Before Matt finished talking, Aubrey was shaking her head. "I can't. I don't want to leave any stone unturned. Every man or woman working on this has a different perspective. We see different possibilities. If I'm not there, what I might have seen in a situation could be the one thing that leads us to the kidnappers."

"You have a point," Matt sighed. "I don't like that you aren't safely tucked away at the ranch, but you have a point." He lowered his head and captured her mouth with his in a brief kiss.

Aubrey's lips tingled where his had touched hers. "Why did you do that?" she asked in a breathless voice.

"Remember, we aren't strangers. Even though we've only known each other for a day and a half, we've experienced a lifetime together."

She smiled up into his eyes. "If you're going to kiss me, kiss me like you mean it." Aubrey leaned up on her toes, wrapped her hand around the back of his neck and kissed him hard, thrusting her tongue past his teeth to caress his.

He gathered her close, pressing his hand to the small of her back, his hips pressing into hers, the ridge beneath the fly of his jeans nudging against her torso.

Fire burned low in Aubrey's belly. If they weren't looking for a missing child... If they were alone in a hotel room...

But they weren't. As much as she wanted the kiss to go on forever, they had work to do. A child needed them.

Aubrey broke the kiss and leaned her head against Matt's chest. "As much as I loved that, can we pick up where we left off later? After we find Isabella?"

Matt hugged her hard against his chest and set her at arm's length. "I'll take a rain check on that kiss. I'm not done with it."

Aubrey smiled. "You're not just saying that?"

"Are you kidding? I'm on fire and no amount of cold showering is going to douse that flame." He led her to her Jeep, frowning at the mess the shooter had made of her back window.

"I'm sorry your Jeep was hit. But I'm glad he

missed you. Do you want to drive, or are you ready for me to take the wheel?"

"After that…" She drew in a shaky breath. "I'm ready for you to take the wheel."

He chuckled. "After that kiss? Or after the explosion?"

"Weren't they one and the same?" She leaned up and brushed her lips across his. "Yup. Definitely an explosion."

He helped her into the passenger side of the Jeep and climbed into the driver's seat.

Aubrey felt comfortable with him driving. "Where are we going?"

"Since we aren't going to the ranch, I thought we'd go driving around."

"Just looking?" she asked, knowing what he had in mind.

"You heard the sheriff," Matt said. "Just looking. We'll note the places we think the DEA and FBI should check out when they get here."

"No contact."

"No contact." He frowned. "And actually, I think we should take my bike. They know your Jeep by now, and I can get my motorcycle in and out of places quickly."

She nodded. "Okay. Let's recon the area and see what we find. That's what you call it, right? Recon?"

"Yes, ma'am."

Chapter Eleven

Matt drove the Jeep to his shop on Main Street a few blocks down from the smoldering gas station. He parked it in an empty bay and got out. The interior of his shop smelled of oil and gasoline. The familiarity of it grounded him.

Aubrey walked around the exterior of her vehicle, shaking her head.

"I can replace that window for the cost of the glass. To get the bullet holes out of the body of the vehicle, you'll have to take it to a body shop."

She sighed. "I'm not worried about it right now, but thanks. And thanks for parking it inside your shop."

Matt nodded. "I'm just thankful you weren't hit. Vehicles can be fixed or replaced. People can't always be fixed. And they can't be replaced."

Aubrey's gaze met his. "No, they can't." She reached for his hand. "I lost several years off my life when I looked in my rearview mirror at the gas pumps exploding."

Matt took her hands in his. "I lost years off my life when I saw that car coming straight at the Jeep with you sitting inside." He exhaled softly. "And then again, when that man started shooting at you. All I could think about was stopping him before he stopped you."

"Once again, you've saved my life," she said. "Thank you." She glanced around. "Mind if I change out of these scrubs?"

"Go right ahead. There's a bathroom through that door." He pointed toward the office.

Aubrey was gone less than five minutes while Matt assessed the damage to the Jeep.

Aubrey had just emerged from the doorway to the office when Matt's cell phone vibrated in his pocket. He fished out the device, glanced at the screen and frowned. "It's Lily."

"Trace's Lily?" Aubrey joined him.

Matt nodded as he pressed the button to receive the call and then put it on speaker. "Hey, Lily. What's up?"

"Matt," she said. "Is Aubrey with you?"

"She is, and I have you on speaker."

"Good. So, you two are all right?" Lily asked.

"We're okay. I suppose you heard about the explosion at the service station." Matt gave Aubrey a crooked smile.

"We did. News travels fast in Whiskey Gulch."

"Yes, it does." Matt frowned. "Is that all you called about? You were just worried about us?"

"Well, yes and no." Lily paused. "Yes, I was worried about you. Right now, you appear to have targets on your backs. That concerns me."

"We're beginning to feel the same," Matt said. He didn't like that idea that they were being watched and tracked and hunted. They'd already come too close to being killed twice.

"I wish I could be out there helping you look," Lily said. "Since I can't be there, I was thinking of who might know where some good hiding places might be in the area."

"And?" Matt prompted.

"You know my father is in prison right now, don't you?" Lily asked.

"We live in Whiskey Gulch. Everyone knows that," Matt said quickly, hoping Lily would get on with her info.

"He knows this area. Probably better than anyone because of his nefarious dealings. He had contacts with other criminals. And he's in prison where he's met more. You might ask him where the cartel members could be hiding a child."

"That's actually a good idea," Aubrey said. "And being on the inside doesn't always mean he doesn't know what's going on outside the prison walls."

"You could call him or, better yet, go see him at the correctional facility," Lily urged. "He's not a dangerous criminal, just a very dishonest man."

"What's he in for?" Aubrey asked.

"Theft, embezzlement and perjury," Lily said. "If you don't like him, don't worry about hurting my feelings. He never was much of a father to me, and he didn't contribute to my upbringing."

"I'm sorry," Aubrey said. "I almost feel guilty that I had a father who was very much a part of my life and set the example of how to live a good life."

"Don't be sorry," Lily said. "Count your blessings. Matt and I would have loved to have had your father in our lives growing up. Alas, you can't choose your parents."

"No, you can't," Matt echoed. "We'll check with your father and see if he can help us identify some hiding places in the area. We're getting more sources with that info, and every little bit helps."

"I hope that helps," Lily said. "And take a pack of cigarettes to barter with. My father never gives anyone anything if he can't get something for it."

"Good to know," Matt said. "Thank you."

"Also, Trace and Irish are out in the county looking for abandoned buildings." Lily sighed. "It's a needle in a haystack approach, but they wanted to do something. They're coordinating with the sheriff to make sure they aren't duplicating efforts. They've divided up the area into quadrants. If you decide to go on your own search, you'll need to tap into their matrix."

"We'll do that," Matt said. "First, we'll hit up your father. He might be able to narrow down our search to a more timely and manageable effort."

"Oh, and Aubrey," Lily said.

Aubrey leaned toward the cell phone. "I'm still here."

"Health and Human Services hasn't come yet. Rosalynn and I are taking good care of the baby. Hopefully, you'll find her sister before they take Mari."

"I hope so," Aubrey said. "I'd like to know they keep the girls together until they get to their uncle's home."

"That's all I have. I'd help, but it's taking both of us to care for this baby since Rosalynn is out of practice, and I'm new at this." Lily chuckled. "It's good practice. I hope to have a couple of babies myself."

"Sooner than later," Rosalynn's voice sounded in the background. "I'm ready to be a grandmother."

"Be safe," Lily said. "See you soon."

Matt ended the call and looked across at Aubrey. "Let's get to the correctional facility and ask those questions. Night will be here soon. If they're going to ship Isabella out, I'd think it would be tonight."

"We can't let that happen," Aubrey said.

"We won't. But we have to find her first." Matt strode toward his bike and handed Aubrey one of the helmets. "We need to make this as quick as possible. The longer we are away, the more chance the cartel has of slipping by those who are watching for them."

He glanced back at her. "Are you up for this? You haven't had any sleep."

"Neither have you," she answered. "I'm fine. I pulled a few all-nighters when I was in college. And I couldn't rest anyway knowing Isabella is still out there."

He nodded. "Exactly how I feel."

"Let's do this." Aubrey pulled the helmet down over her ears and buckled the strap beneath her chin.

Matt did the same, then rolled the bike out of the bay door into the sunshine. After he closed and locked the shop, he swung his leg over the seat and scooted forward.

Aubrey slipped on behind him and wrapped both arms around Matt's middle, holding on tightly.

Matt didn't like that she was exposed on the back. If someone took a shot at them, they'd hit her first. He'd have to be very aware of everything around them. At least they were headed out of the county. The correctional facility was located thirty minutes from Whiskey Gulch. The sun had passed its zenith and was sinking toward the horizon.

After a quick stop at a convenience store to buy cigarettes, Matt pulled out onto the highway and raced toward the facility between Whiskey Gulch and Austin.

He prayed Lily's father knew something about the cartel and where they liked to hide, so everyone could narrow the search. Otherwise, they would have spent an hour of their time for nothing. If Lily's father knew anything, he might save them time and get them straight to the site before they moved her again.

AUBREY'S NERVES TIGHTENED as they parked outside the correctional facility with its chain-link fences topped with strands of barbed wire. She'd never been inside a prison. For a moment, she panicked. What if they went in, and the guards refused to let them back out?

She knew the thought was ridiculous. People were put in prison for crimes they'd committed. Aubrey hadn't committed any crimes. The prison guards had no reason to keep her.

"We're here to see Marcus Davidson," Matt told the guard at the entrance. They had to hand over their driver's licenses. When they were admitted into the building, two more guards, a male and a female, patted them down and led them to a room where they waited for what felt like an eternity. All the while Aubrey twisted her fingers together, worrying about the time that was slipping away from them. They were no closer to finding Isabella.

A handsome man wearing a white T-shirt and white cotton pants with an elastic waistline was led into the room and seated at the table across from Aubrey and Matt. His hair was neatly trimmed and smoothed back from his forehead, and he faced them with a ready smile and ice-blue eyes.

"Matthew Hennessey, it's been a while since I saw you last. You were just a gangly teen struttin' around town like some badass. And who have you brought with you?"

Marcus turned the full force of his charm on Aubrey. "You're a beautiful woman. Prison isn't the place for you. Not that I'm complaining. It's nice to see a friendly female face." His smile appeared genuine and his charisma was unquestionable.

Aubrey could understand why the man had gotten away with so much. He was personable and smooth. Even in prison whites.

His attention returned to Matt. "What brings you to the pokey?"

Matt got straight to the issue. "There's a missing child who might need our help to keep her alive. We hope you can help us."

Marcus raised his hands, palms up. "I don't see how I can help you find a missing person when I'm in here. But I'll humor you." He leaned back in his seat. "What did you have in mind?"

"You daughter said you might know some of the criminal factions in the Whiskey Gulch area and where they like to hide out."

Marcus raised his hands again. "Whoa. I was into embezzlement, not abducting children."

"We don't care what you were into. If you know anything about Los Zetas, the cartel gun-running and trafficking drugs and humans, you might be able to tell us where they like to hole up. We figure we don't have a lot of time."

"Why would you think I'd know anything about the cartel?"

Laying the pack of cigarettes on the table, Matt leaned forward. "That little girl's mother was killed. She has a baby sister and an uncle willing to take them in. You're a father. Would you want your daughter to be sold as a sex slave at four years old to the highest bidder?"

Aubrey studied the man, frustration rising at his indifference. "You weren't a part of your daughter's life, were you? You wouldn't know how terrible it feels to lose your child." Her eyes narrowed. "If you've ever cared about anyone in your life, think about what it would feel like if you lost that person to the cartel. Would you worry that they were torturing her? That they'd use her body up and throw her away like so much trash and leave her broken, beaten body in the woods to be gnawed on by wild animals?" Her voice broke on a sob. "I know what it's like to lose a child. They found mine, battered, broken and dead. I won't let that happen to Isabella. Not now. If you know anything, tell us." Tears streamed down her cheeks. "Please."

Marcus sat back in his chair and clapped his hands. "Bravo. That was one heck of a performance, Ms. Blanchard."

Anger shot through her like a rocket. Aubrey was out of the chair and halfway across the table when Matt grabbed her around the waist and forced her back into her seat.

The guard standing by the door had taken several steps toward them and stopped when he saw that Matt had Aubrey under control.

"He's not worth it," Matt spoke softly in Aubrey's ear. "Come on. Let's get back to Whiskey Gulch. We're wasting our time here."

Aubrey shook with anger at Marcus Davidson's cold indifference. She allowed Matt to help her to her feet. "Lily deserved better than you," she said.

Matt and Aubrey started to step away from the table when Marcus said, "There are a number of places you should look into. If the little girl was taken last night, they're probably getting ready to transport her out of the county and out of the state tonight."

Aubrey's heart turned over. "That's what we're afraid of. We're so desperate to find her, we came to ask you. Sadly, you're our last hope for information."

"Well, you came to the right place. I might just know where you can look." His eyes narrowed. "So, what's in it for me?"

Aubrey slammed her palm on the table, at the end of her patience. "Seriously? You want to barter for a child's life? You're a bigger bastard than I first thought." She straightened and glared at him. "Come on, Matt. I wouldn't trust that his information is worth the time to listen."

"Do you want to find the girl, or not?" Marcus's voice halted her in her tracks.

"You know I do," she said. "I laid my soul bare to make you understand just how much this means to me. Don't toy with me now."

"Have you looked in the old church on the hill to the north of Whiskey Gulch?" he asked.

"As far as I know, the church is not an abandoned building," Matt said. "They still hold services on Sunday."

"And no one goes in there any other day of the week. And it has a large shop building behind the old church they use for summer revivals." Marcus shrugged. "I'd look there first. If she isn't being held there, check out any of the old warehouse buildings down by the railroad."

"The sheriff and his deputies searched those today. They didn't find the girl. He did find a child's hair bow in the old racehorse barn out west of town. We assume it belonged to the girl."

Marcus nodded. "That was another place they've used in the past. The two I just gave you are more likely, depending on timing. Don't give up on them."

"How will they get the girl out of the area if they know the roads have checkpoints?" Aubrey asked.

"Think about it." Marcus's lips twisted into a smirk. "If you can't get out by the road, you look to other modes of transportation."

Aubrey frowned. "ATV? Helicopter? On foot?"

Marcus rolled his eyes. "If they're getting them out of the area altogether, walking and ATVs would take too long going cross-country, and a helicopter would be heard and seen." He shook his head. "What other mode of transportation goes through Whiskey Gulch on a regular basis? One that nobody really notices."

Matt frowned. "The train? But it only stops to load grain from the granary. Otherwise, it moves through without stopping."

"Those are the two most likely places I've known them to go besides the racehorse barn. But it will be tonight. They don't like to sit on their deliveries for too long. It gives the authorities a chance to catch up to them. If the authorities even know they're moving through the area. If they're doing it right, the cartel does trafficking under the cover of darkness. Nobody hears about it or knows what's happening."

Aubrey stared at the man. Horrified. "You knew this was going on and didn't do anything about it?"

Marcus raised his hands. "I like living. So, sue me. Those cartel goons would just as soon shoot you as look at you."

"We'll check out those locations," Matt said. "Anything else?"

"Yeah." Marcus crossed his arms over his chest. "Now you owe me. Let me know when you find the girl. I'll collect on what you owe me then."

Aubrey didn't like his open-ended statement. Lily's words echoed in her mind. The man didn't do something for nothing. "What do you want?"

"I'll let you know when you find the girl." He chuckled. "Don't worry. I won't ask you to kill anyone."

Aubrey clenched her hands into fists. The man was impossible. She could see why Lily didn't have much to do with him. Aubrey thanked her lucky stars she'd had a relatively normal upbringing with parents who loved each other and loved their children.

Lily appeared to be well-balanced, despite her mother being a prostitute and her father being a crook. Aubrey had learned that little bit of gossip early on. She vowed to get to know Lily and Rosalynn better. They were the strong, take-charge type of women she strove to be.

As they left the correctional facility, Aubrey let go of the breath she felt like she'd been holding the entire time she was inside.

"Was it as bad as you thought it would be?" Matt asked.

"Worse." She gave him a weak smile. "Except the part where they let us leave. Going in, I had the uncontrollable feeling that they wouldn't let us back out."

"I know it's ridiculous, but I had that same thought." He handed her a helmet and slipped his on. "Where to first?"

"We should check in with the sheriff, don't you think?" Aubrey fumbled with the buckle.

Matt swept her fingers aside and fastened it for her. Then he brushed his lips across the tip of her nose. "You're cute in a helmet."

Her cheeks heated. "You're just being nice."

"Nope. I call it as I see it." He swung his leg over the seat and scooted forward to give her room.

Aubrey climbed on and pressed her body to his. Riding on the back of a motorcycle required being close and wrapping her arms around him. She liked it. Maybe a little too much for having just met the man. She felt closer to Matt than she ever felt with her first husband. Matt didn't bail on her after a traumatic incident. He stuck with her and made sure she was all right, instead of nursing his own wounds and feeling sorry for himself.

Matt might have been the town bad boy, but Aubrey saw through the front to the man beneath the leather jacket. He had a good heart and he did the right thing, no matter the risk or cost.

She could fall in love with a guy like Matthew Hennessey. Too bad she wasn't ready for another man in her life. Or was she holding back because she was afraid to be hurt again?

Chapter Twelve

Before they reached Whiskey Gulch, Matt slowed the bike and pulled off the side of the road at an intersection. He killed the engine so that Aubrey could hear what he had to say.

"Why are we stopping here?" she asked.

"One of the places Marcus suggested is on this road. We could do a drive-by and report what we see to the sheriff when we get to town. No point taking his people off of other searches until we know more. Are you up for that?"

"Yes," she said.

His eyes narrowed. "On second thought, it might be too dangerous."

"You're talking about the church, aren't you?" Aubrey's brow wrinkled. "I seriously doubt the cartel would hole up in a church. I don't think we'll be in too much danger."

"I hope you're right." He started the engine and made the turn onto the road leading to the Hilltop Church. In less than a mile, they headed up to a rise. At the top stood a small white church with a steeple. As they neared, Matt could see a large building made of metal behind the main structure. It was large enough to hide a truck towing a trailer full of ATVs.

He slowed as they came abreast of the buildings, continuing past until they were out of sight in his rearview mirror. Nobody came out wielding rifles and firing at them. The whole place was eerily quiet.

Aubrey tugged on his arm.

Matt found a spot, out of sight of the church and revival hall, to pull off the road before he turned to find out what Aubrey wanted.

"Can we park the bike and walk back?" Aubrey asked.

"I don't think it's a good idea," Matt said.

"To me, the place appeared to be deserted." Aubrey swiveled on her seat to look behind her. "I don't think anyone is there. But, if there is any evidence that they were here, it might give us a clue as to where we can find them."

"No. They could be lying low. If you poke the hornet's nest, they're likely to come out in swarms."

Aubrey's lips twisted and her brow dipped. "If they aren't there, we can look around, gather what evidence we can find and save the Sheriff another place to check into."

Matt hesitated. The place did look deserted. If they went in on foot, they would have a better chance of seeing without being seen should there actually be someone there. "I'm still thinking this is a bad idea."

Aubrey grinned. "Which means we're going in." She slipped off the back of the motorcycle and started pulling at the strap beneath her chin.

"Yeah. A really bad idea," Matt muttered beneath his breath. Louder, he said. "Let me hide the bike. And when we go in, you have to do what I say, or we turn around and leave right away."

Aubrey stopped fooling with the strap and held up her hand as if swearing in court. "I'll do whatever you say." Then she pulled the strap free and slipped the helmet off her head and shook out her auburn hair.

"Okay, you look cute in the helmet, but even better without it." He winked. "I'll be right back." He pushed the motorcycle off the road onto a rutted track and hid it behind thick brush. When he emerged, he found Aubrey on the other side of the road, staring in the direction of the church though it was out of sight.

"I think we can cut through the woods," she said, "and come up on the side of the metal building. If I wasn't mistaken, it didn't have that many windows."

"It didn't have any windows. Which makes it an even better hideout for someone who doesn't want to be discovered," Matt said. "We'll do like you said and go through the woods. When we get close, we'll hunker down and observe."

She nodded. "Gotcha."

"Tread lightly and keep the talking to a whisper."

Aubrey nodded and fell in step beside him.

They hurried through the woods, moving in the shadows, avoiding the areas of late afternoon sunlight. It wouldn't be long before the sun set, and the cartel would make whatever move they were going to make. They had to find them before that happened. Weeding out yet one more potential hiding place would help to narrow down the playing field.

As they neared the clearing where the church and revival hall were located, Matt put out his arm, stopping Aubrey from moving forward. He pressed a finger to his lips and dropped to a squat beside a tree.

From where they were, they could see the large revival building and the steeple of the church on the other side.

After careful perusal, Matt whispered. "No guard on this side. Stay here and stay low. I'm going to check the other sides. If you hear anything weird, or I don't come back in fifteen minutes, get the hell out of here. Make for the main highway, flag down someone and get to the sheriff's office. Under no circumstances are you to try to find me." He gripped her arms and captured her gaze. "Do you understand?"

She nodded, her eyes wide. "I do." She reached out and cupped his cheek. "Be careful. I kind of like your face." Then she leaned close and pressed her lips to his in a brief kiss.

Matt froze for a second. He hadn't expected her lips on his. Then he tightened his grip on her arms, pulled her close and kissed her hard, his tongue slipping past her teeth to caress hers in a long, slow glide. When he lifted his head, his heart was pounding hard against his ribs and his groin was tight. "Save that for later. I'm not done."

Her lips curled on the corners and she lifted her hand in a mock salute. "Yes, sir."

One more look into her beautiful green eyes and he left her there, moving closer to the building, clinging to the shadows.

The tree line ended twenty feet from the metal building.

For a long moment, Matt studied the perimeter, the shadows of the trees and the corners of the structure. He didn't see movement, nor were there any security cameras that he could identify. Taking a deep breath, he left the cover of the trees and ran toward the building and the shadows it threw.

Once he had his back up against the metal paneling, he moved to the far end away from the structure and peered around the corner. Nothing moved. No sentries stood guard. He ran to the next corner and looked around to the side that faced the church. This side had a set of double doors in the middle of the building. Again no guards, no sign of life.

He listened for voices. All he heard was the sound of birds and insects.

Instead of exposing himself to potential observers who might be hiding out in the church, Matt backed up and circled the building to the other end where another set of double doors allowed entrance to the structure. He tried the door handles, surprised when they turned easily. Standing away from the door, he reached out, turned the knob and pushed the door inward, letting it open slowly, as if carried by the wind.

Matt stood away from the open door, hunkered down in case someone inside decided now was a good time to start shooting.

Again, nothing happened, no sounds, no movement. With his handgun in his palm, he dived into the interior, rolled to his feet and held his gun out in front of him, ready to shoot.

The interior was a cavern of emptiness with

chairs stacked against the walls. At one end of the building was a set of doors and an open window into what appeared to be a kitchen.

Matt hurried through the building, realizing his fifteen minutes were quickly ticking away. If he didn't complete his search quickly, Aubrey would be headed back to the highway and hitching a ride into town.

Still, he was careful not to take anything for granted. He didn't know what was behind the doors at the end of the vast room. He peeked through the open window into the kitchen. It was filled with commercial sinks, refrigerators, stoves and ovens, large enough to feed a lot of people. The door to the right of the kitchen was a pantry lined with shelves and just large enough for one person to get in, grab what they needed and get out. The other door was a utility closet with a hot water heater, a bucket, brooms and mops.

No people were hidden in any of the rooms. As he headed back to the door he'd entered through, he noted the concrete floor had black tire marks as if someone had driven into the building. A dark pool of something slick lay in the middle of the floor between the tire tracks.

Matt bent, touched his finger to the liquid and brought it up to his nose.

Oil.

What had the sheriff said? The barn where he'd found the child's hair bow had oil on the floor.

The cartel had been in this building. Yes, they had been here, but had everyone left?

He headed out the door, ran to the corner and looked across at the church. When he didn't see any movement, he sprinted across to it.

Here, again, the doors weren't locked, and he entered through the main ones. The church was small and simple with a sanctuary filled with wooden pews, a raised dais and a pulpit. Near the entrance on either side were little rooms. They were empty. The church was empty.

The cartel had been here but were now gone.

Matt ran back to where he'd left Aubrey.

"Oh, thank God," she said, and flung her arms around his neck. "I was about to head for the highway." She clung to him for a moment.

He held her close, glad she'd stayed. The thought of her on the highway, hitching a ride, scared him as much as if they'd run into the cartel in the church. For a long moment, he held her close. When they finally backed away, she looked up into his eyes. "You didn't find anyone, did you?"

He shook his head. "No. But they were here. Come on." With her hand in his, he led her back to the revival building and in through the open doors. He showed her the oil spot on the floor and stood looking around, now that he had more time to study the interior.

"Any sign of hostages?" she asked, her voice echoing off the walls.

"No, but I didn't search thoroughly. He walked to the end of the building where the kitchen was and entered through a swinging door, holding the door open for Aubrey.

Aubrey sniffed the air. "Smells like food." She walked to a large rubber trash container and lifted the lid. "Someone helped themselves to some cans of beans and diced fruit." She held up cans that appeared to have been emptied recently. "It's reassuring to know they could be feeding Isabella."

"If it was Isabella they fed," Matt said, his lips pressing together. He walked to the other end of the kitchen and opened a door that led through the pantry and out into the main room.

Aubrey entered behind him. "It was nice of the church to leave the shelves stocked with canned goods. Makes it easy for the coyotes to hole up here. They have what they need to sustain them until they have to move to the next location."

Matt tucked his handgun into his jacket pocket and pulled out his cell phone. "I'll let the sheriff know what we found."

Aubrey grabbed his arm. "Do you hear that?"

Matt tilted his head. The sound of a vehicle coming up the road set off an alarm in his mind. They didn't have time to run out of the building without being seen. The best he could do was get to the door, close it and pray whoever was coming went by without stopping.

"Stay in here," he said, and ran back to the door and eased it closed as a dark truck pulled in behind the church and stopped at the end of the revival building.

Matt raced back across the floor as quietly as he could and dived into the pantry, closing the door behind him as the door to the building opened.

With his heart pounding he peered through the crack he'd left into the dim interior of the revival hall.

Four men entered speaking Spanish, arguing about something. Two carried semiautomatic, military-grade weapons.

Matt muttered a curse under his breath and leaned close to Aubrey. "They're armed. What are they saying?"

"They're mad about the oil on the floor," Aubrey whispered softly in Matt's ear.

One of the men shoved another toward the end of the room where Matt and Aubrey were hiding.

"He told him to get something to clean it up," Aubrey said. "What are we going to do?"

"The mops are on the other side."

Aubrey touched his arm. "He's headed this way."

Matt backed her into the corner niche and pressed his body to hers, praying his black jacket and jeans would be enough to hide them when the man looked into the pantry and realized he was in the wrong room.

He fit his hand into his jacket pocket and gripped his pistol. If he had to, he could fire through the leather. With four men to deal with between them and their exit, he preferred not having to make a move. Maybe the men would leave without knowing the two of them were here in there first place.

With his face close to hers, he could feel the warmth of her breath on his neck.

"I'm scared," she whispered.

Footsteps sounded outside the door to the pantry.

When the door was flung open, Aubrey opened her mouth on a gasp.

Matt covered her lips with his, stifling the sound, praying the man would see he had the wrong room and move on to the other door.

Voices sounded in the revival hall.

The man at the door shouted back to them in Spanish.

For what felt like an eternity, the door was

open. The dim light from the hall's interior cut across the floor of the pantry, almost to where Matt and Aubrey stood flattened to the wall behind a shelf of canned goods.

Then the door slammed closed and the footsteps led away from the room to the other side of the kitchen.

More words were spoken in Spanish, now muffled by the closed door.

Matt remained where he was, his body pressed to Aubrey's, waiting until the voices stopped and the men left the revival hall.

Minutes passed like hours.

The door at the other end of the kitchen opened and closed. A little while later another door closed farther away, on the other end of the hall.

When silence once again reigned, Matt leaned back and whispered. "I think they're gone."

Aubrey's hands rested against his chest, her fingers digging into his T-shirt. "They are?"

He nodded, reluctant to move much farther. While he'd been leaning into her body, his own reacted to her nearness. His groin was tight, and his body burned for this woman.

Surrounded by darkness, all he could do was feel the way her chest rose and fell, her firm breasts pressing against his chest with each breath.

"Matt?" she whispered.

"Yes, Aubrey?" His pocketed his gun and slid his hands up her arms to cup the back of her neck.

"Are they really gone?"

"I think so." He rested his lips on her forehead. "At least for now. Let's wait a bit to make sure they're gone for good. I'll text the sheriff, though."

He pulled his phone up and sent a quick message to the sheriff about their location, what they'd observed, the area the ATVers were in. He got a fast response telling them not to pursue, that the sheriff's office would take care of it. When he was finished, he looked into Aubrey's eyes.

"If the sheriff can cut them off, maybe we'll get Isabella sooner than we thought."

"You said to save that kiss for later." Her whisper grew softer. "Is it later?"

"I believe it is." Matt buried his fingers in her hair and tugged, tilting her head back. He swept his mouth over her cheeks and down to her lips, feeling his way, tasting her skin as he went. When their lips collided, there was no going back. He had to kiss her, hold her, feel her body against his.

He pressed her back into the niche, her back

against the wall, his hands on her, his tongue inside her mouth.

Aubrey curled her calf around the back of his and pressed her core against his thigh.

Matt groaned. "What is it about you that's driving me out of my mind?"

"I had that same thought," she said into his mouth, their breaths mingling, their tongues sliding against each other.

"We should go," he said.

"We should," Aubrey agreed, her fingers curling into his shirt, dragging it out of the waistband of his jeans.

"And we will," he said, his hands finding the hem of her blouse and pulling it upward, his knuckles skimming across her bare skin. Fire burning through his veins.

She raised her hands above her head, her breasts jutting into his chest.

He pulled off her blouse and draped it over cans stacked on the shelf beside them. Still working in the dark, he found the button on the front of her jeans and flicked it open.

Aubrey pushed his leather jacket over his shoulders and laid it on the ground by his ankles, the gun in the pocket thunking against the concrete. Then she was back to his shirt dragging it up over his chest and shoulders. He helped her get it over his head and added it to where he'd left her shirt on the stack of cans.

Matt couldn't believe he was in a dark closet, stripping this stranger, who wasn't a stranger at all. He swept his hands over her back, found the clasps on the back of her bra and released them. She shimmied out of the straps, letting it fall to the floor between them.

Then it was a frenetic struggle to get her out of her shoes, jeans and panties.

Standing before him, naked in the dark, she cupped his crotch, still covered in denim, and squeezed lightly. "You're overdressed for this clandestine operation," she whispered.

"That can be remedied," he said. When he reached for the zipper on his jeans, she brushed his hand aside and lowered it herself.

His erection sprang free into the palm of her hand. He'd gone commando. She smiled, wrapped her fingers around him and slid her hand down his length.

Matt tensed.

She let go of him and wrapped her hands around his hips, sliding her fingers beneath the denim to capture his buttocks in her hands. Pulling him closer, she rubbed the furry mound of her center against his staff, while shoving his jeans down to his thighs.

He grabbed the wallet out of his back pocket,

flicked it open and dug inside, praying he had protection stored there. When his fingers contacted the foil packet, he let go of the breath he'd been holding. With his teeth, he tore open the pouch and handed the condom to her.

She rolled it over him with both hands and downward, until he was fully encased. Aubrey placed her hands over his shoulders.

Matt bent, his hands circled her thighs and he lifted her up, wrapping her legs around his waist. He captured one of her breasts between his teeth and rolled the tip until it firmed into a tight bead. Flicking it with his tongue, he made her moan and arch her back, forcing more of the luscious mound into his mouth. He obliged, sucking in as much as he could.

He lowered her slowly until his staff pressed against her entrance, nudging her. "Are you sure?"

She moaned. "Yessss." Aubrey lowered herself onto him, taking him fully into her slick channel.

Matt eased into her until he was fully sheathed and held steady, allowing her to adjust to his girth. She was so tight, wet and warm.

Aubrey raised up on him and lowered herself down again.

He pressed her against the wall and slid in and out, increasing the rhythm of his thrusts until he was pumping in and out of her.

Tension built and spread throughout his body until he could contain himself no longer. Matt shot over the edge, his shaft pulsing with his release.

Her palms captured his face and tilted it upward. Her lips found his in the darkness and she kissed him while she rode him all the way through to the end.

He held her tight, kissing her, making love to her, wishing it could go on forever.

A sound outside the door made him freeze.

"Did you hear that?" Aubrey whispered so softly only he could hear.

"I did." He lifted her off him and set her on her feet. Then he zipped his jeans and bent to retrieve the gun out of the pocket of his leather jacket.

Easing the door open a crack, he looked out into the revival hall.

Nothing stirred. No one moved.

With the little light coming through the crack in the door, he retrieved their clothes, handing Aubrey's to her.

He threw on his shirt and jacket and returned to the crack in the door. "Stay here," he whispered.

Matt slipped out of the back of the pantry into the kitchen and pushed through the swinging door into the open bay of the revival hall. A mop lay on the floor near the wall. It hadn't been there when Matt and Aubrey had come through earlier. It had a dark oily residue on the strands' cotton coils.

The oil spill in the middle of the floor was gone, along with the black tire tracks.

Matt moved along the wall to the opposite end of the building and nudged the door open. The yard surrounding the revival hall and the church was empty. The men were gone, leaving them alone.

Matt returned to the pantry.

Aubrey was fully clothed, peering out of the crack in the door.

"All clear," he said. "They're gone."

She fell into his arms. "I don't like it when you go off without me."

"I don't like leaving you," he said, holding her close. "But I'd rather you stayed safe than catch a bullet."

"And I'd rather this was all over and we could lead a normal life." She buried her face in his shirt for another moment and then straightened. "It'll be getting dark soon. We need to get to the sheriff and see if they've made any progress."

"Here's hoping they've picked up their trail."

"I'm afraid for that little girl. We have to find her tonight. Otherwise, they could take her anywhere and we'd never find her."

He tipped her chin up. "We'll find her. I promise," he said, praying he could keep that promise. "And when this all over, we'll get to that normal life you talk about. As long as normal includes me seeing you again."

She smiled and laid her hand on his cheek. "Somehow, I don't see a life with you being all that normal. And I'm okay with that. A few less bullets would be nice, but I'll risk some of those, as long as I get to see you again."

He kissed her briefly on the lips. "You're on."

They exited the revival hall and hurried back to where they'd left the motorcycle hidden in the bush.

Matt wasn't sure how they'd find the little girl or where. The only thing he was one hundred percent sure of was that he wanted to see Aubrey again. What they'd just experienced was the beginning of something big. Something he never thought he'd ever have in his life. A connection so deep he was willing to risk his life to be with her.

Chapter Thirteen

Aubrey wrapped her arms around Matt's waist and pressed her body against his as she rode back to Whiskey Gulch on the back of his motorcycle.

What had just happened back there at the church was something she hadn't expected and would never have dreamed of. With the ink barely dry on her divorce papers, she'd just made love to a man after coming close to being discovered and possibly killed.

The fear and the exhilaration of living through the terror had heightened her desire. Never in her marriage had she ever made love like that, standing in a darkened pantry, overcome with longing. Nor had she made love anywhere else but in a bedroom.

Sex against the wall was… Amazing.

Her arms tightened around the man who'd taken her to the next level of intimacy. There was so much more she wanted to do with him, but they had a mission to accomplish, a child to reunite with her sister and uncle. Their focus had to be on the task at hand, not on making love in the pantry of a revival hall.

She was deliciously sore, her nipples were tender and she was achy in all the right places. All those feelings had to be set aside as they pulled into the parking lot of the sheriff's office.

Several sheriff's service vehicles were parked there, as well.

Aubrey dismounted and waited for Matt to join her. He held out his hand. She took it and they walked into the sheriff's office together.

The sheriff stood in the front of the office, talking to Deputy Jones and another deputy Aubrey didn't know, but had seen in town.

When the sheriff saw them, he waved them forward. "Hennessey, Ms. Blanchard, I'm glad you're here."

"Have you had any luck locating the cartel hideout?" Matt asked. "Did you bring in the ATVers?"

The sheriff frowned. "I sent some unmarked cars out to the location you gave us, and they came up empty. Those men know this area and must have used off-road trails. We're still on it, though." He huffed out a sigh before continuing.

"I spoke with Trace Travis. He said you'd made a trip out to the correctional facility to see Marcus Davidson. Was he of any assistance?"

"Maybe," Matt said.

"He gave us two possible locations," Aubrey said. "One we've already checked out."

Matt picked up the story, filling in the details he'd left out of his text message. "The Hilltop Church north of town. We went there and discovered they'd been there, as I told you. Like you noted from the racehorse barn, the truck they'd been using leaked oil. There was a puddle of oil in the revival hall and black tire marks on the concrete. While we were there, four men speaking Spanish showed up and cleaned up the oil and tire tracks."

"Anything indicating the girl was there or with them?"

Aubrey's cheeks burned. They hadn't followed the men because they'd been busy making love in the pantry. Now she wished they'd gone after the crew instead of trusting the sheriff's office to find them.

"No," Matt answered. "They were heavily armed and all I had was a handgun. We waited until they left and came straight here after I sent you the text."

The sheriff nodded, acknowledging that was the right course of action.

"Marcus said they'd probably be shipping their cargo out tonight," Aubrey said. "However they decide to do it. He suspects it will be by train."

"Since you have all of the highways being watched coming in and going out of the area, it makes the most sense," Matt said.

The sheriff nodded again. "Then all I need to do is put my people on the train track and stop any trains leaving here until we inspect each car."

Matt frowned. "Sounds too easy. I can't imagine anything going that smoothly. These guys have been operating in the area for a while. I think that's why my mother was murdered. She was providing a hiding place for those who got loose from the cartel trafficking. They shut her down."

"And if you continue to hinder their operation," the sheriff said, "they'll try to shut you two down, as well." He shook his head." You might want to step back from this case."

Matt's lips firmed. "Can't."

Aubrey slipped her hand into his. "Won't. If there's a way we can help free that little girl, we're going to do it."

"Okay then. I'll position a few more of my people on the railroad tracks. There are a couple of abandoned buildings at the old switchyard. I'll personally lead a team through to see if they've staged their cargo. In the meantime, why don't you get some rest? You must be exhausted."

Matt shook his head and squeezed Aubrey's

hand. "We'll grab a bite to eat at the diner and get back out to look for Isabella."

"Okay," the sheriff said. "Let me know where you're heading so my guys don't mistake you for the cartel and shoot you."

"Thank you, sir." Matt said.

Aubrey waited until they were outside of the sheriff's office before she said, "I'm not really hungry."

"You might not be, but I am." He smiled. "I'll get a burger to go. We can split it and eat it as we're driving through the county looking for abandoned buildings."

She glanced at the sun slipping into the horizon and sinking lower by the minute. "We don't have much time left. They're going to make their move tonight. I feel it."

"Me too," he said.

They mounted his motorcycle and headed to the diner, where Matt ordered a hamburger cut in half to take with them.

They had just stepped outside the diner into the shadowy gray of dusk, when a loud explosion shook the ground. A plume of smoke and fire rose from the southern end of town.

Matt reached his arm around Aubrey and pulled her close, his heart pounding against his ribs. Loud sounds like that reminded him too much of his days in Iraq and Afghanistan as a member of Marine Force Recon. Flashbacks of attacks and being under siege made his pulse race uncontrollably.

"Isn't that the direction of your mother's house?" Aubrey's voice brought him back to Whiskey Gulch, Texas. He wasn't in the Middle East, nor was he in Marine Force Recon anymore.

Matt studied the direction of the rising smoke. "Yes it is."

"Do you think…" Aubrey's voice trailed off.

"That the cartel have targeted the house of angels again?" His jaw firmed and lips pressed into a tight line. "I wouldn't put it past them."

"Why?" Aubrey's eyes filled.

"As a warning?"

"Your mother's place was lovely and peaceful." Aubrey grabbed for her helmet and slipped it over her head.

"Before the coyotes and the cartel discovered it was sheltering people they'd targeted." Matt jammed on his helmet and straddled the motorcycle. He patiently waited for Aubrey to get on with him.

She slid her leg over the back, wrapped her arms around his waist and held on as Matt raced through town. As she neared Maple Street, her heart sank. She knew it would be the place she'd called home for the past few months. But the reality of seeing Matt's mother's home burn to the ground was more difficult knowing Matt was seeing it, too.

Matt stopped at the end of the street, far enough out of range of the flames and any more explosions that could occur whether set by the cartel or the gas line igniting.

Aubrey dismounted the motorcycle and pulled off the helmet.

Matt did the same and stood staring at the demise of a part of his childhood.

Aubrey slipped her hand through the crook of his elbow and pressed her cheek against his shoulder. "I'm so sorry."

"It's just a house," he said, his voice rough like he'd swallowed gravel.

She nodded, knowing it was much more than just a house. It held memories of his mother and their lives together.

The wail of sirens sounded from the fire station and soon the fire engine and rescue trucks arrived. Aubrey stayed by the motorcycle while Matt crossed to the first responders.

The roar of the fire burning and the rumble of the fire engine truck drowned out the sound of other engines until too late.

Three ATVs burst out of the woods and raced straight for Aubrey.

She turned in time to see them heading for her.

Aubrey took off running, heading toward Matt and the firefighters.

One of the ATV riders cut her off, reached out and grabbed her arm. He yanked her off-balance, turned into her and pulled her across his lap.

Aubrey flailed and screamed but couldn't find leverage to push herself up or roll out of the man's grip.

His partners fired shots from their weapons and flanked the ATV with Aubrey on it.

Aubrey tried to scream and kick but lying on her belly across the man's lap and the ATV gas tank meant that every bump they hit, the air was knocked from her lungs.

She was carried away from the burning building, into the woods as darkness cloaked the land. One particularly hard bump made her head hit something solid. Her vision blurred and finally blended into the blackness around her.

WHEN AUBREY'S SCREAM sounded over the noise of the fire engine, burning inferno and men shouting instructions, Matt turned back to where he'd left her, standing by his motorcycle.

That's when the men on ATVs stormed in, grabbed her and took off, firing their military-grade rifles into the crowd of first responders.

"Get down!" Matt cried out. While the others dropped to the ground, Matt ran toward the men taking Aubrey. He headed straight for them, regardless of their weapons. He didn't give a damn if they shot him. Aubrey was his concern. They had her and they would kill her if he didn't get her back immediately. He couldn't fire his handgun at them for fear of hitting Aubrey.

No matter how fast he ran, their four-wheelers were faster, taking them into the shadows of the woods. He continued running until he could see them no more.

His lungs burned with the need to breathe and his muscles screamed at how hard he'd pushed. He bent over, dragging in deep lungfuls of air, cursing and hating himself for leaving her alone for even a minute. She was gone, and he'd let it happen.

Matt pulled out his cell phone and called 911. "Get me the sheriff. Now!"

The dispatcher patched him into the sheriff's number.

"They blew up my house on Maple Street."

"I wondered what the explosion was all about," the sheriff responded.

"Sheriff, they got Aubrey."

The sheriff swore. "We're on our way in from the rail yard."

"What good does it do to come to the fire? They took her into the woods. We have to find where they're hiding before they kill her. You know they will." After doing horrible things to her first, he thought, his stomach turning at the idea.

"We're on our way. We'll track them through the woods. We'll find her."

Matt wasn't so sure. He ended the call and hit the speed dial for Trace. When his brother answered, he said, "I need your help."

"You've got it," Trace said.

"They have Aubrey."

"We're on our way into town," Trace said. "Where should we meet?"

"Maple Street. They blew up my mother's house."

"Are you okay?" Trace asked.

"No. They have Aubrey," Matt said. "Nothing's okay." He ended the call and walked back to his motorcycle.

Five minutes later, the sheriff arrived in his service vehicle followed by an unmarked dark sedan.

The sheriff and deputy got out and hurried toward Matt as two men in street clothes exited the dark sedan and joined him.

"Matthew Hennessey, this is FBI Special Agent Mitch McCall and DEA agent Will Knowlton." He turned to the fire. "They set up a distraction."

"Seems extreme to go to all this trouble to kidnap a woman."

Will Knowlton shook his head. "They're sending a message to anyone who might consider helping their human product escape, as well as those who are considering escape."

"Well, their message now includes the abduction of a woman who didn't even know she was living in the house of angels." Matt paced away from them and back. "What do you know about these people?"

"Just that they're known for being very ruthless, I'm sorry to say. We've been monitoring their trafficking patterns," Agent McCall said. "They have a kind of corridor through this area. The coyotes bring the product, whether its drugs or people, across the border and hand off here."

"We haven't discovered who they're working with on this side to hand off to. That's the missing link," Knowlton said. "If we could find him, we could stop the transfers. They'd be hard-pressed to sell what they have without a go-between."

"Do you know where they're hiding their 'product'?" Matt asked.

Knowlton and McCall both shook their heads.

Matt clenched his fists. "Then what good are you to me?"

"They're extra sets of eyes to help in our

search," the sheriff said. "I have every one of my deputies on duty and spread across the county. They're instructed to stop everyone and inspect every inch of every vehicle."

"They were on ATVs. Unless they transfer her over to something else, they aren't on the roads. Did you find anything at the train yard?"

The sheriff shook his head. "Nothing."

Minutes later, Trace, Irish and Lily arrived in Trace's pickup, followed by another truck he didn't recognize with another man Matt didn't know.

Trace and Lily brought the man with them over to where Matt and the others were congregating. "Matt, this is Levi, the guy I told you about from my old unit. He just arrived today, fresh off active duty to come to work with our Outrider organization," Trace said.

Levi held out his hand. "Nice to meet you."

"Same. Is there a chance you can see in the dark and track ATVs for miles? I could really use someone like that about now," Matt sighed. "They have Aubrey and they'll kill her. Members of cartels don't like to be humiliated by a female and they don't like it when someone takes what they think belongs to them." He led them to where the ATVs had disappeared into the woods. "They could be miles away by now." A rush of hopelessness threatened to overwhelm him. "We haven't discovered where they're hiding yet. How are we going to do it now in the dark?"

Levi nodded. "I have a collection of night vision goggles."

"We'd have to get close enough to humans for them to be of any use. Until we locate their hideout, we don't have a starting point."

"I also have a drone with a heat signature camera," Levi said. "It's one of my hobbies I just picked up during my time off."

Matt perked up. "Did you bring it with you?"

Levi nodded. "It's in my truck."

"Can you get it up and running?"

"Sure," Levi said. "Give me a few minutes."

"The fewer minutes, the better. They already have a twenty-minute head start. I don't know what good the drone will be, but it's better than nothing at this point." Matt ran a hand through his hair. "I don't have any idea where to start. Between me and Aubrey and the sheriff's folks, we've checked a lot of the abandoned buildings in the area and found nothing."

"What about the buildings that aren't abandoned?" Knowlton asked. "These people aren't moving through this area without help."

"They've been hiding a truck and trailer that can haul ATVs," Lily said. "Who has a place big enough for them to drive the entire rig inside?"

"There's a number of barns in the area." Deputy Jones planted her fists on her hips, frowning. "Who would be most likely to help the cartel?"

"We don't have enough support staff to block the roads and check all the potential hideouts at the same time," the sheriff said.

"You have us," Knowlton said, jerking his thumb from himself to Special Agent McCall.

"And us," Matt said. "We can't stand around doing nothing. We have to look everywhere we can."

"What about the aluminum boat factory?" Trace said. "I was in there as a kid. They have room inside that place to park several boats. That would be enough room for a truck and trailer."

"There's the auto body shop, car dealership, storage units and the old five-and-dime store," Deputy Jones said as she ticked off on her fingers. "Didn't Rodney Morrison purchase the old shoe factory to renovate and make into apartments?"

"As far as I know, he hasn't started the renovation," the sheriff said. "It's big enough to hide a truck and trailer inside. All of those places could have been used."

"All of this takes time," Matt said. "That's what we don't have a lot of."

Knowlton, McCall, Irish, Trace, Levi and Matt exchanged phone numbers with each other and Sheriff Richards.

"Keep in mind, these guys are deadly mean and armed to the teeth," Matt reminded them. "They've already tried to kill us twice."

Levi hurried to his truck, returned with the drone and laid it out on the ground. With the joystick in his hands, he started the engine and sent it up into the sky. "I'll keep you all informed of any movement I detect of a truck and trailer, or anything that could be used to transport people. I know what to look for."

"Good," Matt said. "I'll take the storage units and the old shoe factory since they're on the same road."

"Lily, Irish and I will look into the auto body shop, car dealership and the five-and-dime," Trace said.

"I'll work with McCall and Knowlton to give them directions to the barns I can recall are large enough to hide a truck and trailer," Sheriff Richards said.

"Call before trying to go into any place and be careful," the sheriff added.

"Let's go." Matt strapped Aubrey's helmet to the back of his motorcycle and pulled his helmet down over his head. His heart pinched hard in his chest. This was his fault. He should have kept her closer to his side. They'd tried twice now to kill her. He should be glad they hadn't just driven by and shot her. He held out hope they'd find her before the cartel hurt her. If they were lucky, the cartel planned on selling her into the sex trade. He almost laughed at the thought that he could be glad they wanted to sell her. That would give them time to find and free her. The alternative was that they would kill her and dump her body in a ditch somewhere.

He would never forgive himself if that happened. After what they'd already been through together, he wasn't ready for it to end. He liked her. A lot. He could see them dating and maybe... More.

Damn it. They would have that opportunity, if it was the last thing he did.

Chapter Fourteen

Aubrey came to when the four-wheeler she was draped over slowed to a stop. She was dumped unceremoniously on the ground, hitting her head and shoulder hard. Pain shot through her temple and arm. For a moment she lay stunned.

Men spoke Spanish, arguing over who would tie her wrists and ankles. Someone was supposed to be there and hadn't arrived. They couldn't stay long, or the police would find them.

All their words floated through Aubrey's head, the translation garbled at best. She wasn't sure who they were waiting for.

As her head cleared, she knew she had to get out of there, fast. She pretended to be unconscious, studying the terrain. They'd stopped on the side of a dirt road, hovering in the deep shadows of the trees. If she could get up and run, she might be able to elude them and duck out of sight until they gave up looking for her.

Aubrey counted to three in her head, then

rolled to her belly, bunched her knees beneath her and launched herself away from the three men, two of whom were still on their ATVs.

She ran for the deepest darkest point in the woods where she hoped she could hide until they moved on. The problem with going for darkness was she couldn't see the obstacles in her path. She tripped over a branch, falling to her knees. On the ground for only a second, she pushed to her feet and ran again.

Behind her the men shouted. The three guys on the ATVs circled around and raced after her, headlights penetrating the darkness, finding her and making straight for her. Their lights helped her to find her way, but not to hide from them.

Aubrey darted to the right. Her night vision compromised by the ATV headlights, she ran into a briar bush, the thorns catching her clothes and skin, bringing her to an abrupt and painful halt. She backed away, her clothes snagged and her skin torn, but she made it out and ran another direction.

The men on the ATVs caught up with her and cut off her escape, circling her like a pack of wolves. One of them dived from his machine and tackled her, knocking her to the ground. The weight of his body pinned her. Facedown in the dirt, her breathing ragged and her skin bleeding, she struggled but couldn't shake the man from her back.

Another man approached. In the light from the ATV's headlights, Aubrey could see that he carried a syringe.

"No!" she said, fighting twice as hard. At one point, she managed to move the man on her back, but not enough to escape.

The needle was jammed into her arm and something burned as it entered her bloodstream.

In the next moment, the world spun and whirled, the lights making her dizzy. The weight on her back lifted. She could breathe better, but she couldn't move a single muscle. All of them were as limp as wet pasta. Lying in the dirt, drooling, all she could think was that she wanted to see Matt again.

Hands gripped her arms and dragged her across the ground toward the road. A white van stood there with the door open.

Aubrey wanted to fight, to free herself, but she couldn't muster a single ounce of energy. Even if she did, she wouldn't know which way to run when her world spun in all directions. She squeezed her eyes shut, hoping the spinning motion would subside. Instead of fixing her problem, she'd magnified it to epic proportions. She wanted to put her foot over the side of the bed like she had when she came home after a night of drinking. At least then, she could stop the room from spinning.

Whatever they'd given her had drained her completely and sapped from her body any strength she might have used to get away. The two men swung her up into the van and dropped her on the floor. Her head bounced, but she didn't really feel it. She lay like a pile of rags on the floor of the vehicle, feeling very disconnected from her body. A man with salt-and-pepper hair spoke in Spanish to the men who'd brought her there on the ATV. Money exchanged hands and the ATVs departed.

Her head swimming in and out of consciousness, Aubrey was vaguely aware of the van moving along the dirt road and out onto a paved road. They bumped over something hard on the road twice and didn't go much farther before the van pulled into something dark like a cave.

She could hear the sound of an overhead door closing behind them.

The van door slid open, hands grabbed her under her arms and by the ankles and dragged her out, depositing her, none too softly, on a concrete floor. She lay next to what appeared to be a dog kennel.

The sound of sniffling came from inside the kennel.

Aubrey's head lay beside the grated gate of the

kennel. The room was dark, but when someone opened one of the doors on the front of the van, enough light spilled out, allowing Aubrey to see into the kennel.

Instead of a dog, the dull eyes of a child shone out of the darkness. She sat hunched over, her dark hair matted, her body smelling of urine. She was dirty, grimy and terrified.

And Aubrey could do nothing to help her.

She tried to move her hands. If she was moving them, she couldn't feel it. She focused her brain on wiggling her toes. Again, she couldn't feel the toes wiggling.

Even opening her mouth to talk was impossible. She lay completely helpless and unable to do anything for the child in the cage.

The child whimpered and stuck her fingers through the grate, touching Aubrey's hair. "*Ayudame, por favor*," she whispered. Help me, please.

Aubrey lay beside the little girl they'd spent the day searching for. She wanted to say something to reassure the child that she would be okay. Not only could she not say a word, she wasn't sure she could lie to the girl when she didn't know if they would make it out of wherever they were alive.

A man walked around the van and stood over her. Because she couldn't move her head, all she could see were the toes of his wing tip black shoes. Aubrey knew the voice, but her foggy brain was having a hard time placing it. She'd heard it that day. Where?

The man with the voice squatted down beside her. "Because you meddled in my business, you cost me a lot of money and credibility with my contact." He glanced at his watch. "Fortunately, the trade of you for that baby will make up for some of it. Guess you won't be needing a house in Whiskey Gulch after all."

That was it. The real estate guy in the diner. Rodney something or other. Morrison. Aubrey blinked her eyes, the only part of her that would respond to her mental command. Her fingers were tingling but still wouldn't move. Her toes were beginning to have a little feeling in them.

"Ten minutes. That's all we need. Ten minutes and you two are on your way to your new lives."

"Bas...tard," she forced past her heavy tongue.

Rodney laughed. "Yeah, but I'll have the last laugh at your expense. You've caused enough trouble in this town. I had free run after I got rid of that Hennessey woman. I'll be damned if I let you pick up where she left off with the house of angels. She cost me too much profit."

"Won't...get...away...with this," she said, slowly getting her tongue under control.

"I can, and I will," he said. "You won't be

around to squeal on me. You'll be in a dirty brothel in some city, providing entertainment to men who are willing to pay the price. You and that dirty thing." He nodded toward the girl in the kennel. "What men see in little girls is beyond me. They're filthy and smell."

When you keep them in kennels like dogs, they're going to be dirty and smell. Aubrey didn't bother voicing her opinion. The man wasn't human. No real man would sell women and children into the illegal sex trade. Clearly, all Rodney was concerned about was the money involved in the exchange.

Aubrey willed strength into her arms and legs. But no amount of positive thinking would chase the effects of the drug they hit her with. Time was the only cure. And time was something she didn't have a lot of.

Rodney Morrison straightened and called out an order in Spanish.

Two men converged on her, flipped her onto her stomach, wrapped her wrists in duct tape behind her back and secured her ankles.

Lying on her belly, her face turned toward the kennel, she could still see the little girl.

The sound of a train whistle blasted nearby.

Aubrey could feel the rumble of the heavy train grow as it moved closer.

Was this it? Was she going to be sold into the

sex trade, drugged, tied and unable to fight her way free? She was so close to Isabella, and yet, she could do nothing to help the child. No little girl should have to go through what Rodney Morrison had in mind for them.

Aubrey focused on her fingers. The tingling had spread from the tips into her hands. She flexed her fingers, the feeling starting to come back. At the rate it was returning, they'd be loaded onto the train and gone before she could figure out a way to get out of the tape binding her.

Since her divorce, she'd prided herself on her independence. And, normally, she could handle most situations. But, right at the moment, she needed a miracle. Or a hero.

She looked at the little girl in the kennel and said in Spanish, "*Todo saldrá bien. Viene ayuda.*" It'll be all right. Help is coming.

She prayed she was right. The sheriff and others had focused on the train. Were they still doing that or had they started chasing other leads?

"Come on, Matt," she whispered. "It's up to you now. Find us."

MATT'S GUT KNOTTED as he rode his motorcycle to the first place on his list. The storage unit was on his way, so he pulled in there first. A quick drive around the metal buildings convinced him this wasn't the place. The only unit large enough to drive a truck into with a trailer on it wasn't even locked. He got off his bike, pulled his gun and rolled the overhead door up.

The unit was empty. In the field beside the storage units were motorhomes and trailers parked until their owners were ready to take them out on the road. Just to be sure he wasn't missing anything, Matt drove past the larger recreational vehicles, shining his flashlight, to make certain no one had parked a truck and trailer among them.

Again. Nothing.

Without wasting another second on the location, he shot back out on the road to the old shoe factory on the north end of town. He knew the roads and took some shortcuts he'd learned as a teen, driving through an alley behind several commercial buildings to get to the old factory.

He stopped behind a building that had been a butcher shop back when he'd been a kid. The shop had been closed for years, and the building was boarded up. Matt killed the engine and turned off the headlight, parking the bike in the shadows. From there, he continued on foot.

The shoe factory was just far enough out of town to be secluded, but close enough most people wouldn't have considered it a logical place to hide a truck and trailer. Then again, the paved road wasn't the only one that went to the factory. A dirt road led into the woods behind the building and out to another farm-to-market road, if he remembered correctly. He'd thrown his share of rocks at the windows in his youth and run into the woods when he thought someone was after him. No one cared about the building and it had fallen into disrepair even back then.

If Morrison had purchased the factory to convert into apartments, he had yet to start the work and it would take a sizable investment of capital to make something of the old brick building. Morrison must have been making bank on real estate to think he could sink more money into the place. He'd be better off bulldozing it and starting over.

Matt swung wide, approaching the shoe factory from the side away from the main road leading in. As he moved closer, the hairs on the back of his neck prickled.

Call it intuition, or gut feeling, something wasn't right at the old shoe factory. With his weapon drawn, he eased up to the building, searching for a window or door. In the center of the building was a single door that led out the back of the long structure. All the windows were above his head. He'd have to climb up on something to look in.

Matt headed for the door, moving in the shadows of the trees that had overgrown the property. When he was parallel with the door, he crossed the area open to the starlight shining down, ducking back into the shadow of the structure.

Once he reached the door, he turned the knob slowly, praying it was unlocked.

It didn't turn all the way, nor did it open.

Muttering a silent curse, he debated going around to the end of the building. Both ends and the front of the building would be exposed to the starlight and would be the direction anyone keeping watch would expect someone to come from.

Matt looked through the clutter of broken pallets and building debris for something he could pile up to stand and gaze into the windows. He found an old barrel turned on its side.

Careful not to make a lot of noise, he rolled the barrel to the side of the building and turned it up on its end. He pressed on the metal top. It was rusty but should hold his weight.

Matt climbed onto it, testing the strength of the rusted metal. Balancing most of his weight on the rim, he straightened and attempted to look into the building.

The glass was so dirty, he couldn't see through. Matt rubbed at a spot until he'd cleared enough grime to get a view. When he could finally see inside, he had to give his vision a moment to adjust to the even darker interior.

Shadows took shape and his gut clenched. Up against the wall closest to the front of the building was a stack of lumber. On the other side of the stack was something covered in what appeared to be plastic sheeting or tarps. The shape was tall enough and long enough to be a pickup with a trailer on the back.

Matt could detect no other movement inside, nor could he see anyone standing guard. He dropped down off the barrel and ran to the end of the building and looked for sentries posted to keep people out.

No one.

He tried the door on that side. It was locked. Hurrying to the front, he checked again, knowing already that the place was deserted. They'd parked the truck and trailer the ATVs had been brought in on and left.

On the off chance they'd left their prisoners inside with the truck, Matt tried the door on the front of the building. It was locked.

The time he'd already spent on this location was time they could be getting Aubrey and Isabella out of the county.

Past caring how much noise he made, he kicked the door. The old lock gave, and the door swung open.

Matt ran inside, weapon drawn, checking all four corners for movement. As he suspected, no one was there. He went straight to the plastic sheeting, ripping it away to expose a truck and a trailer big enough to haul the ATVs. Why would they leave the truck and trailer unprotected? Unless they planned to abandon them and take another mode of transportation out of the area.

Running back to his motorcycle, he pulled his cell phone out of his pocket and called the sheriff. "I found the truck and trailer they used to haul the ATVs in the old shoe factory."

"Anyone there with them?"

"No. It's as if they abandoned them for now."

"I'll put out an APB to pick up Rodney Morrison."

"What else does Morrison own or have access to?" Matt asked.

"He has a number of places throughout the county. Rental houses, commercial buildings he has leased out."

The long, loud wail of a train whistle sounded, sending a ripple of fear through Matt. Marcus Davidson's words came back to him. They'd go out by helicopter or by train. "What does Morrison own along the railroad track?"

"I'm not sure," Sheriff Richards said. "We checked the buildings by the rail yard earlier. We didn't find anyone in them."

"That was at the rail yard. What about the granary and the old rail depot?"

"We were looking for a place large enough to house the truck and trailer," the sheriff said. "Besides, the granary is still a working operation. It would be hard to use it for something like trafficking. I'm not sure who owns the depot now. It hasn't been in service since the seventies."

"Does someone check on the granary every day? Or only when they have grain to load on a train?" Matt asked.

"Only when there's grain being loaded into the silos or onto a train," the sheriff said.

"How long does the train stop in Whiskey Gulch?" Matt asked.

"Not long, if they haven't prearranged grain operations or cargo to be loaded." The sheriff paused. "Look, I'll start looking at the north end of the row of buildings along the track," the sheriff said.

"I'll start at the south end near the depot and granary," Matt said. "And I'll notify my team."

"I'll let my deputies know not to shoot you and your guys."

As Matt ended the call with the sheriff, he reached the place he'd left his motorcycle. He called Trace and let him know what he'd found at the shoe factory.

"The train is rolling into town now," Trace said. "If they don't have cargo scheduled, they might move on through. Either way, the train will be slowing enough someone could possibly get on, even if they don't stop. I'm coming down the tracks from the north. If you join me, keep in mind that train will be out of town before we have much of a chance to search the cars."

"Headed there now," Matt said, swinging his leg over his bike. "Will take me about three minutes."

"You'll get here sooner than we will. We're on the opposite end of town."

"I'll be the guy moving around in the shadows. Don't shoot me," Matt said.

Trace chuckled. "I wouldn't dream of shooting the half brother who horned in on my inheritance."

"Not making me feel much better," Matt grumbled.

"You're family now. We're on our way."

"Out here." Matt pulled on his helmet, revved the engine and spun out of the alley onto the road. Time was ticking by. If he wasn't right about the train… Thirty minutes had already passed since Aubrey was taken. If her abductors had slipped past all the roadblocks, they could be miles away by now.

Laying open the throttle, he raced toward the railroad, praying he wasn't too late.

Chapter Fifteen

The drug was wearing off. What started as tingling in her fingertips and toes spread to her hands, feet, arms and legs. Soon she was able to move her entire body. Unable to break, by sheer force, the duct tape they'd used to bind her wrists, she had to find something sharp to rub it against that would cut through the tape.

The room was dimly lit by the glow of starlight through a window.

Morrison stood with two Hispanic men, watching out the window, speaking in low tones, their backs to Aubrey.

Able to move now, she turned her head and scanned the area, looking for something sharp. She lay on a tile floor in what appeared to be an office of some sort with an old metal desk and a file cabinet in one corner.

The loud blast of a train whistle gave their location away. The building they were in had to be near the railroad tracks, and Morrison and his cohorts were staging their human products for transport.

Hope surged inside Aubrey.

After their conversation with Marcus Davidson, Matt would know to check the train coming through town that night.

Aubrey couldn't wait for him to find her. What if he'd been injured in the fire at his mother's cottage? The sheriff had been responsible for checking the buildings along the railroad tracks. If he'd already verified they were empty, would he think it worth their efforts to check again?

The cartel knew their business, including how to hide human cargo by keeping it moving from place to place. Hadn't they seen that already by the evidence of the oil in the racehorse barn and the revival building?

Aubrey frowned. Where had they hidden the leaky truck and the trailer? She'd been brought here in a van. Matt and the sheriff weren't looking for a van. They were looking for the truck. Had Morrison and his cartel groupies ditched the truck as another way to distract the searchers?

While the men were staring out the window, Aubrey eyed the old metal desk. It was hard to tell whether there were any sharp edges on the desk, but, as far as she could tell in the gloom, it was her only chance of finding a surface to scrape the tape against.

She rocked her body, testing the movement for the noise it might create. So far, her efforts had drawn no attention from her captors. They were looking through the window, probably watching for the coming train.

Another loud whistle sounded.

Based on the deafening blast, the train was getting closer. If she didn't do something soon, she would have no chance to break through the duct tape before they tossed her and Isabella onto the train, taking them to some buyer intent on using them in the sex trade.

Aubrey had no intention of letting that happen to her or Isabella. But, if she was going to be successful, she couldn't let them hit her up with whatever drug they'd used on her in the first place. She'd been completely incapacitated. Aubrey had never been more frightened in her life. Women and young girls were being forced into doing things they would never do by being given drugs that diminished their physical and mental capacity.

She wouldn't let that happen. Couldn't.

Matt, his friends and the sheriff's department would find them before it was too late.

Aubrey glanced at the men by the window again. Their focus was outside the window; they weren't paying attention to her.

She rocked one direction and rolled back in the

other direction as hard as she could to get over her bound hands. She rolled again and ended up with her back to the metal desk. Moving like an inchworm, she positioned her hands against one of the legs on the desk, felt for a sharp edge and nearly cried when she found one.

Quickly and quietly, she sawed her hands back and forth, rubbing the duct tape against the sharp and rusty metal desk leg. She couldn't tell if it was working or how close she was to breaking through.

The next train whistle sounded so loudly, the train had to be right outside the building.

The men at the window turned suddenly.

Aubrey went limp, closing her eyes, pretending she was still unconscious.

Two men lifted the crate containing Isabella and carried it out the door.

Two other men frowned as they moved toward Aubrey. Had they noticed that she'd moved?

Her eyes cracked open just enough to see through the slits, Aubrey watched, wishing she was free to fight against the men grabbing her by her arms and feet. The duct tape held true as they carried her outside. She'd not been able to cut it.

A bright light headed their way, slowing as it neared where they were standing. The metal on metal sound of the train wheels rolling on the tracks grew louder and louder.

Come on, Matt, Aubrey willed.

Cars rolled past, one by one, the train lurching to a crawl, a pace slow enough that a man could walk alongside and keep up.

One of the men ran down the line of cars, jumped up on one of them and pulled open a sliding door.

As it passed where they were standing, two men tossed the crate containing Isabella into the car with the man who'd opened the door. Another man jumped in with the little girl.

No.

Tears filled Aubrey's eyes. She'd promised Isabella that help would come.

But it hadn't. Now it was up to Aubrey to save the little girl.

She didn't struggle to get loose. Now was not the time to miss the train that was taking a child away to be sold into misery. Aubrey studied the car they'd thrown Isabella into. Graffiti covered the exterior with a skull and some letters she couldn't quite make out in the dark. She counted the number of cars as they passed.

Another man ran down the track, jumped onto the side of the train, slid open the door on one of the empty cars and dived inside.

Morrison and the dark-haired guy beside him lifted Aubrey beneath her arms and by her ankles and swung her up into the open car.

She landed so hard, it knocked the breath from her lungs and shot pain through her hip and shoulder where they hit the floor.

As she lay on her side regaining her breath, the train rumbled beneath her. She twisted her hands, pulling hard, working the tape she'd already torn a little. The man who'd dived into the car before her reached out a hand and helped the dark-haired man who'd aided Morrison when he threw her in.

He pulled the other man up into the car.

Morrison didn't join them. That meant she had to deal with only two men.

Only. She fought the urge to laugh hysterically. Her best bet was to pretend to be unconscious and get the tape off her wrists and ankles. Once she freed herself, she'd figure out how to get past the men and up four cars to free Isabella. She wasn't leaving the train without the girl.

While the two men stood by the door, looking out at the buildings as they passed slowly, Aubrey rolled over to the other side of the car and rubbed the tape on her wrists against the rusty wall, pulling hard against her wrists to break the tape. She could feel the strands snapping one at a time.

Finally, her wrists broke free.

Her glance went to the two men. They still stood at the door, looking out.

Aubrey struggled to remove the rest of the

tape from her wrists and then brought her knees to her chest and worked at the tape around her ankles. The noise of the train rolling across the tracks masked the sound of her unwinding the tape from her ankles.

When she was free, she looked again at the men standing at the door like bowling pins ready to be knocked over. She had one shot at getting this right. Bunching her legs beneath her, she launched herself at the man closest to her like a linebacker going for the quarterback. She hit him hard in the middle of his back. He pitched forward into the other guy, and they both fell out of the rail car.

Aubrey caught herself on the side of the door, struggling to avoid falling out of the train after the two men.

A shout sounded outside the train. The two men she'd shoved were on their feet and running alongside, catching up to the car where Aubrey clung.

One of them pulled out a gun and aimed it at the car.

Aubrey threw herself to the floor. A second later, the crack of gunfire sounded, and a bullet pinged against the railcar.

The train continued to move slowly. The men racing after it were catching up to the car she was in. Her plan to free herself and get rid of the men hadn't included them coming back.

Chapter Sixteen

Matt arrived at the granary at the north end of Whiskey Gulch and drove past the silos, one at a time, looking for movement, vehicles and people. He didn't see anything out of place. When he arrived at the office building, he parked his bike and moved up to it, his weapon drawn, past caring if he was seen. Their time was running out.

The train had reached the south end of town and was rumbling slowly through. If the cartel planned on moving people on the train, they'd be somewhere along the tracks, waiting for the chance to load them onto a car.

He looked into the windows of the office. No one moved inside. The place appeared deserted.

With the train moving closer, he didn't have time to waste. He returned to his motorcycle and left the granary, moving on to the depot at least two hundred yards ahead.

As he approached the old building that had long since been retired and sold, the engines of a long cargo train chugged along the railroad track, passing the depot and the granary where Matt had been moments before.

His pulse picking up, Matt opened up the throttle and raced toward the depot.

The train wasn't slowing to a stop. If Isabella and Aubrey's abductors were going to get them on that train, they'd have to do it while it was moving. They could have already done it from one of the buildings along the track farther north of the depot. Which meant, Aubrey and Isabella could be in one of the cars passing Matt as he raced toward the other building he was supposed to check.

A white van pulled away as Matt arrived at the depot.

Matt couldn't let anyone leave the area without being questioned. He caught up to the van, drove alongside the vehicle and pounded on the window. "Pull over!" he shouted.

The driver slowed to a stop and the window came down. Rodney Morrison stared out at him, an eyebrow cocked. "Matthew Hennessey, what are you doing terrorizing law-abiding citizens in the middle of the night?"

"Where is she?" Matt demanded.

Morrison's brow wrinkled. "Where is who?"

"Don't play dumb with me. We found the truck

and trailer you've used to haul the ATVs around. They're in your old shoe factory."

Morrison blinked. "I have no idea what you're talking about. I rarely go into the old shoe factory. I don't currently have the funds to start work on the property at this time. Why should I bother to go there?"

"To hide the truck and trailer used to haul the ATVs around." Matt glared at the man. "Where are Aubrey and Isabella? I know you're in this up to your eyeballs. Tell me where they are, and maybe the judge will go easy on you."

Morrison's eyes narrowed. "I told you. I don't know what you're talking about. The last I saw Ms. Blanchard, she was with you at the diner. Maybe the sheriff should be looking at you for her disappearance. You were always the delinquent in Whiskey Gulch."

Anger roiled in Matt's gut. "You're not going to get away with this."

"I've had enough of your accusations. If you have a problem with me, speak to my attorney." The van surged forward.

Deep down, Matt knew Morrison had to be involved in the abductions and the cartel's human and drug trafficking in the area. He couldn't let Morrison get away, and he couldn't take the time to wait for the others to catch up to him.

The van pulled away from where Matt sat on his motorcycle.

To slow Morrison down and to keep him from leaving the area in a hurry, Matt did the only thing he could think of. He raced after the van, swerved his motorcycle in front of it at the same time as he threw himself off the bike. He hit the ground hard, rolled away from the wheels and came back up on his feet.

The van hit the bike, rolled over it and high-centered on the machine, coming to a complete stop with a jerk. Morrison's head slammed against the steering wheel and he lay still.

Behind Matt, the train gave another long, loud hoot, pulling him back to what really mattered. Morrison was the least of his worries. Aubrey and Isabella could be on that train. Since Morrison was at the depot, he had to have been involved. The two had to be on the train that was still moving slowly down the track on its way out of town.

On foot now, Matt raced toward the tracks, pulling his cell phone out of his pocket as he ran. The screen was cracked, but the phone worked. He called the sheriff. "Morrison's crashed in a white van by the depot," Matt blurted out. "He's involved. I'm running for the train and could use some backup. Try and get someone to stop the train. I think the girls are on it."

"Gotcha," Sheriff Richards said. "Headed that way. I'll send one of my deputies to secure Morrison."

As soon as he ended the call, Matt hit the number for his half brother, Trace. "Depot. Now."

Trace didn't question. "On our way."

Matt reached the tracks and looked toward the north. Already, half the train had moved through town and was headed out the other end. If Morrison had loaded the girls onto the train, as Matt suspected, they'd be on one of the cars near the front. The part of the train now passing the granary was moving farther away.

Ahead, he could see the silhouettes of two people running alongside a railcar, trying to get in. One waved something in his hand. The next moment, Matt heard the sound of gunfire.

He picked up his pace, drawing on the training, strength and endurance he'd needed as a member of Marine Force Recon. An old leg injury hurt him significantly, especially after purposely crashing his motorcycle, but he fought past the pain to reach Aubrey and Isabella before the two men could get onto the train.

As soon as Matt got close enough, he came to a dead stop, aimed his handgun and fired. The man pointing his weapon into the boxcar fell to the ground. The other man spun and fired at Matt.

Matt anticipated the move and dropped to a

crouch, aimed and fired at the second guy and missed.

The man fired back at him.

Matt had already ducked. The bullet went wide.

Before he could fire again, the man grabbed the side of the train and swung up inside.

Matt raced for the boxcar the men had been trying to get into.

When he reached the door, he grabbed the edge and hauled himself inside.

A woman cried out and the sounds of a scuffle came from the shadows.

As Matt straightened, a dark, bulky silhouette emerged and lurched toward him.

Aubrey came into the starlight. The man who'd leaped onto the train had a gun to her head. "Oh, Matt," she said. "I tried."

Her captor spoke in rapid-fire Spanish, tipping his head toward the gun in Matt's hand.

Matt didn't understand what he said, but his intent was clear. If Matt didn't put down his weapon, the man would shoot Aubrey.

"Don't worry about me," Aubrey said. "Isabella is in the fifth car up from here. Save her."

The man holding Aubrey spoke again, jerking his head toward the door.

"He wants you off the train," she said. "Go, Matt. Help that little girl."

"I'm not leaving you," Matt bit out.

Her captor pulled her hair, making her head tip upward. He yelled in Spanish.

"You can't wait," Aubrey said, her tone strained. "They might kill her. And he said if you don't get out, he'll kill me. Please. Go."

Matt fought with his desire to rush forward and deck the man threatening to kill Aubrey. But the man held all the cards. He had Aubrey.

He couldn't risk Aubrey's life. If he left, what was to keep the man from shooting Aubrey to be done with her before getting away?

As he contemplated how to maneuver so he could reach for the weapon before the man fired, the train jerked, throwing all three of them off balance.

Aubrey jabbed her elbow into her captor's gut, broke free and threw herself across the floor of the railcar.

Her captor regained his balance and swore in Spanish, and once again aimed his handgun at Aubrey.

Matt raised his weapon and shot him.

The man staggered backward. His gun fell from his hand as he dropped to the floor, clutching his chest. He lay still.

Matt kicked the gun away from the man and then helped Aubrey to her feet and into his arms. "I'm sorry, I failed you."

"What are you talking about?" She shook her head. "You didn't fail me. Who would have thought they'd risk being caught to capture me?" She clung to him for a moment. "Besides, I knew you'd come."

"We haven't known each other long…" he started.

She smiled. "But it feels like a lifetime."

"I could very easily fall in love with you, Aubrey Blanchard." He kissed the tip of her nose and then claimed her mouth in a brief but earthshaking connection. "I think I already have."

She kissed him back and then leaned her forehead against his chest. "I could fall in love with you, too, Matthew Hennessey."

The train was slowing.

Aubrey broke away. "Isabella."

"Five cars up?" Matt confirmed.

Aubrey nodded. "Yes."

Matt hugged her close again and then set her at arm's length, took her hand and walked to the open door of the boxcar.

As they looked out, the train came to an excruciatingly slow halt.

Matt jumped to the ground and held up his arms to help Aubrey down.

She leaned forward and let him lower her to her feet. Her body trembled in his arms and his chest tightened. This woman had come so close to death.

The sheriff's vehicles arrived, along with Trace's truck. Everyone jumped out and rushed toward Matt.

"Fifth car up from here," Matt said.

"See anyone leave the car?" the sheriff asked.

"Not from this side," Aubrey said.

"They'll probably use the little girl as a hostage to get away," the sheriff said.

"Can you use us?" Trace asked.

"One of you serve as a sniper in the military?" Sheriff Richards asked.

Irish stepped forward, his rifle with the scope in hand. "I did."

Sheriff Richards nodded. "Deputy Jones was on the rifle team in the army. I'll set her up on this side. You can take the other."

Irish ducked between two railcars and hurried forward with two of the sheriff's deputies.

The sheriff pulled a megaphone out of the front seat of his vehicle and called out. "Exit the boxcar with your hands up."

A shout sounded from the other side of the train. One of the sheriff's deputies slipped between the cars and called out, "Door's open on this side, they're gone and there's an empty dog crate in the car!"

"Isabella was in that crate," Aubrey said, her face draining of color.

Matt turned to Lily. "Will you take Aubrey to Trace's truck and keep her safe?"

Lily nodded and held up her handgun. "We've got this. I won't let anything happen to her. Come on, Aubrey. Let these guys do what they were trained to do."

Aubrey's gaze met Matt's. "I promised Isabella she'd be okay."

Matt nodded. "I'll bring her back." He cupped the back of her head and pressed a kiss to her lips. "Levi still have that drone in the air?"

Trace nodded and held up his cell phone. "He's flying it over us right now. I have him on speaker."

Levi's voice came over the cell phone. "I have heat signatures for two, heading east from your position. One of them appears to be carrying a child."

"Let's go." Matt took off with Trace, Irish, the sheriff and his deputies, passing between the boxcars, heading east, with Levi on speaker guiding their way.

Matt hoped Lily and Aubrey made it back to Trace's truck and that the cartel didn't have more of their people hanging around the depot. He had to trust that the fierce spitfire Lily would keep Aubrey safe with the one weapon between them.

"One hundred yards to your east," Levi reported. "You're closing in on them."

"I'm going to fire a warning shot over their heads," the sheriff said. He raised his handgun and fired off a round. Then he lifted the megaphone to his lips. "Stop and come out with your hands up."

"Are they stopping?" Trace asked Levi on the cell phone as they continued toward the fugitives.

"No," Levi said over the phone.

The sheriff handed the megaphone to Deputy Jones. "In Spanish."

"Yes, sir." She took the megaphone and repeated the sheriff's message in Spanish.

"What are they doing?" Trace asked Levi.

"Still moving... No, wait. They've stopped. No, now they're moving. It appears they've left the child behind."

"Is she moving?" Matt asked.

"She's sitting in one spot," Levi reported. "I can't tell what her condition is."

"The men?" Sheriff Richards asked.

"Moving fast, heading southeast."

"Get us to the child," Matt said.

"You're still headed in the right direction. Another fifty yards."

Matt ran through the woods and brush, dodging trees he could barely see in the darkness. Trace ran on one side of him, Irish on the other.

"Maybe ten yards," Levi said.

"Isabella!" Matt called out. "Isabella!"

He stopped yelling and listened.

"You should see her…now."

Matt scanned the ground, searching for the little girl.

"There!" Irish shouted and pointed to a bush three feet in front Matt.

Matt circled the bush and looked down.

A small child with long black hair sat in the grass, sniffling.

When Matt reached for her, she scooted back into the brush.

Matt spoke to her in soft, soothing tones like his mother had when he'd been scared as a child. "Hey, Isabella, sweet little girl, I'm not going to hurt you. I'm going to take you to see your sister, Marianna."

Her eyes widened, the whites showing in the starlight. "Marianna?" she said in a tiny voice.

Matt nodded. *"Si, Marianna."*

"Y mamá?" And mama?

He couldn't answer her question about her mother, so he repeated. *"Si, Marianna."* This time, when he reached for her, she let him take her into his arms.

Isabella wrapped her own arms around his neck and clung to him.

"Do you want me to take her?" Deputy Jones asked, holding out her hands.

"No," Matt said. "She seems fine for now." He stroked the hair on her head and talked softly in her ear. "It's going to be all right. We're going to see your sister, Marianna."

He looked around for the others.

Deputy Jones was the only one with him. "The rest have gone after the two men who ditched the girl," she said. "Let's get back to the vehicles and get this poor baby someplace safe and warm."

"I know just the spot."

"Child services will want to take her."

"They can collect her when they come to get Marianna. I promised Isabella we were going to see her sister. And, if they haven't already come to collect her, Marianna is at Whiskey Gulch Ranch with my stepmother."

"I'll escort you there."

"Good, because I seem to be without trans-portation," He doubted his motorcycle would be repairable. Frankly, he didn't care. Isabella was okay. Aubrey was okay. The dark spot on the en-tire scenario was that the two little girls would be without their mother, all because of a cartel more interested in money than human lives. The bastards needed to be stopped.

Matt walked back to the depot with Deputy Jones. As they approached the vehicles, Lily and

Aubrey dropped down from Trace's truck and ran toward them.

Matt's chest swelled and his face broke out in a grin.

Aubrey wrapped her arms around Matt and Isabella, happy tears trailing down her cheeks. "You're going to be okay. *Vas a estar bien.*"

Isabella wrapped one of her arms around Aubrey, retaining her hold on Matt.

"You're going to be okay," Aubrey repeated.

Matt believed her. Seeing Aubrey come toward him, her arms outstretched had given him the feeling of coming home. He hadn't had that feeling since he'd returned to Whiskey Gulch. It took an angel to bring him home.

Chapter Seventeen

The ride back to the Whiskey Gulch Ranch was strange. Aubrey rode with Matt and Isabella in the back of Deputy Jones's service vehicle.

Isabella remained in Matt's arms the entire way. Aubrey smiled at the little girl's reluctance to let go of him. The big, tough-looking bad boy of Whiskey Gulch had charmed yet another female into loving him.

Aubrey couldn't blame Isabella. Matt was a handsome man with his black hair, much like Isabella's, and piercing dark eyes.

"Deputy Bateman called an ambulance for our friend Rodney Morrison," Deputy Jones said through the wire mesh between the front and the backseat of the SUV.

Her heart pinching hard in her chest, Aubrey touched Matt's hand. "It was Morrison who killed your mother," she whispered, not wanting to wake the child. "He admitted to me that he'd gotten rid of her because she was meddling in his business."

"Had I known it was him, I'd have made him suffer more," Matt said through clenched teeth. "So, he was there when they loaded you on the train?"

Aubrey nodded. "He was the man in charge of the men doing the dirty work."

Matt's nostrils flared. "I had a hunch when I saw him driving away from the depot in a white van."

Aubrey grunted. "The van he had his goons transfer me into after they shot me up with some drug. I was paralyzed for thirty to forty-five minutes."

Swearing softly, Matt squeezed her hand. "I'm sorry you had to go through that."

"The worst part of being drugged was knowing everything that was going on, and not being able to do a thing about it." Aubrey leaned against Matt's shoulder and held his hand. "They kept this poor child in a dog crate, and I couldn't lift a finger to get her out. Even after the drug wore off, I was bound with duct tape. I'd only just begun working it loose when they tossed us onto the train."

Matt released her hand and slipped his arm around her shoulder. "It's over now. You're here with me, and I won't let anyone hurt you."

Deputy Jones's radio crackled, and Sheriff Richards's voice came across. "We got the two men. Wouldn't have been able to do it without help from our men and women in uniform and our former military men who stepped up to the challenge. Tell Ms. Blanchard and Mr. Hennessey thank you for all they did to bring these coyotes to justice."

Deputy Jones responded. "Glad to hear it, sir. I'll let them know." She leaned her head toward the back of the vehicle. "Did you hear what the sheriff had to say?"

"Yes, ma'am," Matt said. "The combined effort of all those involved made this mission a success."

"I wish all investigations had such a positive outcome," Deputy Jones said. "Gotta celebrate the good ones and learn from the others." She chuckled. "At least that's what my boss says."

"Aubrey?" Matt said.

Her heart fluttered at her name on his lips. "Yes, Matt?"

"You think we could stand each other when we're not in a crisis?"

She laughed. "Do *you?*"

He smiled and brushed his knuckles across her cheek. "I think we make a great team, crisis or not." His smile faded. "Aubrey Blanchard, will you go out with me? I'm pretty sure I love you and I need time to convince you that I'm not all that bad."

She leaned into his palm. "Mr. Hennessey, I can't think of anything I'd like better. I'm already convinced you're perfect and I'm more than half-way in love with you."

"When we get young Isabella settled down for the night with her sister, Marianna," Matt said, "I'll show you just how serious I am."

After the trauma of the past couple of days, seeing the light side of Matt was refreshing and utterly endearing. Aubrey cocked an eyebrow, loving teasing him. "Promise?"

"Promise." He adjusted Isabella against his shoulder. "How do you feel about kids? I mean, I know you lost your daughter. And I can't begin to imagine all the heartache that goes along with that."

She touched his arm. "I love children," she said, softly, past the lump in her throat.

"Me too." Matt tilted his head toward the child sleeping on his shoulder. "If she didn't have an uncle waiting for her and her sister, I'd be tempted to adopt them."

"We could ask the uncle if he's interested in letting the girls come live with us." Aubrey winked. "That is, if this dating thing pans out."

Matt stared at her with a crooked smile. "You would do that?"

She nodded. "The thought of these girls being motherless breaks my heart. My Katie would have loved sisters to play with." Tears welled in Aubrey's eyes as she laid a hand on Isabella's hair. "They are as different as night and day, but they want and need the same things—a safe home, love and family."

"A family with a mother and father who care about them," Matt said, his gaze going to the child in his arms and then up to connect with Aubrey's. "You just made me love you even more."

A big sigh sounded from the front of the SUV. "You two are making me think my life isn't as good as it could be. Could you cut it out before you make me go all soft?" Deputy Jones shook her head. "You'd think the only way to be happy around here is to be in love and have a dozen kids. I like being single and doing my own thing."

Aubrey laughed and brushed the tears from her cheeks. "Dallas, you do you. It's what you do best."

"Whew," the deputy said with a sigh. "I was worried I'd be held to another standard."

"Not at all. You just haven't met the right one," Aubrey said, staring over Isabella's head to Matt. "When you do, you'll be willing to move heaven and earth—"

"Or reconsider your single status," Matt concluded with a smile. "I know I am."

"I'll say. Going footloose and fancy free to having a woman and two children is a huge step," Deputy Jones said. "I don't know if I could handle that much change all at once."

"You'll know when you know." Matt reached for Aubrey's hand as the SUV turned into the gate at the Whiskey Gulch Ranch.

Aubrey knew, and by the look in Matt's eyes, he did, too.

Epilogue

Matt sat on the porch swing at his home at Whiskey Gulch Ranch with Aubrey beside him, holding baby Marianna in her lap. Isabella sat on the floor of the porch with a kitten they'd found in the barn, teasing it with a feather. The dark-haired little girl giggled when the kitten grabbed for the feather and missed.

For a child who'd lost her mother days earlier and had been abducted and shoved into a dog crate, she was adjusting better than could be expected.

Her uncle had asked to be given time to think about what to do with Isabella and Marianna. He had five children of his own to support and was living paycheck to paycheck. He'd loved his sister, but he knew the children were better off where they were. They'd have a roof over their heads and wouldn't have to share a room with three or four other kids.

Every once in a while, Matt thought it was a

huge step, taking on two small children when he wasn't even married and didn't have a house of his own. But he'd started working with a local architect on house plans. And he'd been in discussions with Trace about a location for that house on the Whiskey Gulch Ranch. Since they'd inherited the huge ranch together, they'd come to an understanding and were building mutual respect for each other.

Matt and Aubrey had found a beautiful spot on a knoll overlooking a small lake not far from the original homestead where Trace and his mother lived. They'd have their privacy and be close enough for Rosalynn to spoil her bonus grandchildren, as she called Isabella and Marianna. With her big heart and open arms, she was well on her way to loving the beautiful baby girls.

And Aubrey had taken to the orphans so quickly, it was obvious she was a natural.

Today they were celebrating Isabella and Marianna's uncle's decision to let the girls stay at the ranch while he considered whether he could shoulder the extra responsibility. Trace and Lily were manning the grill, cooking large steaks from the beef they raised on the ranch. Irish and Levi were throwing horseshoes on the lawn and smack-talking about their skills in everything from sharpshooting to poker.

Rosalynn was busy in the kitchen preparing

her famous potato salad and baked beans to go with the steaks.

Sheriff Richards and his wife arrived with their little girl, bringing along Deputy Jones with them. Another vehicle arrived behind them and FBI Special Agent Mitch McCall and DEA agent Will Knowlton emerged.

"Just in time for dinner," Trace called out from the grill.

Mrs. Richards laughed. "My husband has impeccable timing when it comes to steak."

The sheriff set his daughter on the ground and rubbed his flat belly. "A man's got to have his priorities."

His wife patted his back. "I know, dear. And tuna casserole isn't one of them."

"Did I say that?" The sheriff hugged his wife. "You make the best tuna casserole of any I've ever tasted." He kissed the top of her head. "Can I help it that after twelve years of marriage, I still don't like tuna casserole?"

The sheriff's daughter settled on the porch with Isabella and the kitten.

Matt chuckled and pulled Aubrey close. "Is that what we're going to be like when we've been married for twelve years?"

"I don't know. We have to be married before we can start the countdown to twelve years," she said.

"You're right. We do." He looked over at her and opened his mouth to ask her to marry him.

Aubrey held up her hand before he could. "Don't. Not yet. Ask me in two weeks."

"Careful, brother. Two weeks might give her time to change her mind," Trace said as he walked up the steps carrying a tray loaded with juicy steaks. "She might decide she doesn't like riding around on the back of a motorcycle all the time."

Aubrey shook her head. "No. I know what I want and what I'm getting into. I've been married and know what it takes to raise children." She cocked an eyebrow. "Matt needs at least two weeks, maybe more, to change *his* mind. Taking on a woman with the baggage I have, plus two little girls is a lot for a confirmed bachelor to manage. He needs to think hard on it before he commits."

"Darlin', I've thought on it. I know what I want." He kissed the top of her head. "I want you." Then he touched the baby in her arms. "And Marianna and Isabella." He sighed. "But I'll give you the time you need to be sure that I'm sure." He winked.

"That will give him time to find a ring and do it up right," Lily said.

Levi and Irish joined them on the porch.

"What do you hear from Morrison?" Levi asked.

"In a plea bargain, he confessed to everything, including his role in the death of Lynn Hennessey," said FBI Special Agent McCall.

Matt's lip curled. "What kind of plea bargain is he getting?" The man deserved the death sentence.

"He won't get the death sentence as long as he helps identify the cartel members he's worked with in the US and the women and children they've sold in their trade dealings." The sheriff held up a hand. "We will push for life without parole. The man has no business being on the streets. Not with all he's done and the lives he's impacted. But if we can stop the flow of human trafficking in this area, we can save so many more lives."

"He gave us a lead we'll be following on his US connection." Deputy Jones tipped her head toward agents McCall and Knowlton. "We'll be working closely with the FBI and DEA to bring those guys down."

"Deputy Jones will be working the case," Sheriff Richards said.

"I'd like to be involved, if you could use some assistance," Irish said.

"We'll keep you in mind," Agent McCall said.

"Waiting to see if Morrison's information leads to anything."

"Keep us in mind," Trace said. "I'm bringing on more of the men I served with on active duty. We plan on taking on more than just ranch work. Me, Matt, Irish and Levi are just the beginning of a team of former military men who can work to help others."

The sheriff frowned. "We don't need vigilantes running amok."

Trace smiled. "We're not vigilantes but we want to help where we can. And we're willing to augment or assist other agencies in their efforts, at no cost to those agencies."

"Good to know," Sheriff Richards said. "Now, where's that steak?" He gathered his daughter and carried her inside.

Irish held the door open for Deputy Jones, laughing at something she said as they entered.

Matt remained in the porch swing with Aubrey. He tipped his head toward Irish. "Think those two could work together?"

"I don't know them well enough to say. Irish seems to enjoy Dallas's company. He was pretty quick to volunteer to help out on the case."

"Are you hungry?" Matt was perfectly happy to sit there with the three women who were going to be his family, but he had to take care of them and see to their needs.

"As much as I love sitting here with you and Marianna, I could stand a bite of steak and Isabella needs to eat. She could use some meat on her little bones."

"Then let's get our girl something to eat." He pushed to his feet and helped Aubrey and the baby out of the swing. He held her in his arms and kissed her forehead, the baby pressed lightly between them. "You're my own angel from the house of angels."

"What are we going to do about your mother's house?"

"It's gone. The fire destroyed it."

"Are we going to rebuild it?"

He shook his head. "I have what I need from the house in my memories of my mother and you. If not for that house, we wouldn't have Isabella and Marianna. I'll never forget it, but we have an entire life ahead of us here on Whiskey Gulch Ranch. And as long as we have each other, we will be okay."

Aubrey leaned up on her toes and kissed his lips. "More than okay." She smiled. "Did I tell you that Mrs. Blair is going to be the fourth in the ladies' poker games?"

"Ol' Mrs. Blair?"

"I asked Marge and Barb if they would be willing to invite her to play, and they said yes."

Aubrey frowned. "Do you think Mrs. Blair can keep up with them?"

Matt snorted. "Keep up? Are you kidding? She'll be beating the socks off them in no time."

He bent to scoop the little girl into his arms. "Isabella, are you hungry? *Tienes hambre*?"

"*Si. Muy hambriento.*" She laughed as she settled into his arms.

Matt couldn't remember a time he was happier. He smiled all the way into the house with his three girls at his side.

* * * * *

Get 4 FREE REWARDS!

We'll send you 2 FREE Books plus 2 FREE Mystery Gifts.

Harlequin Romantic Suspense books are heart-racing page-turners with unexpected plot twists and irresistible chemistry that will keep you guessing to the very end.

FREE
Value Over
$20

Get 4 FREE REWARDS!

We'll send you 2 FREE Books
plus 2 FREE Mystery Gifts.

Harlequin Presents books feature the glamorous lives of royals and billionaires in a world of exotic locations, where passion knows no bounds.

FREE
Value Over
$20

Get 4 FREE REWARDS!

We'll send you 2 FREE Books plus 2 FREE Mystery Gifts.

FREE Value Over **$20**

Both the **Romance** and **Suspense** collections feature compelling novels written by many of today's bestselling authors.